"It is so predictable. I've heard it all before. 'You're just a woman. What could you possibly know?' Over and over."

"Why do you put up with it?" Lon asked. "You should be taken seriously."

Mercy sighed. "Human nature is funny. Even when confronted by the truth about the cause of the epidemic, the average male and most females refuse to believe a woman would know more than a man would."

"But your idea about the cause of cholera is based on what male doctors have discovered, isn't it?"

She nodded. "But I could have gotten it wrong. I am, after all, just a poor, inferior, weak female who must always defer to men, who *always* know better than women do."

Her words grated against his nerves like sandpaper on sensitive skin. Why? Was he guilty of thinking this, too? How many people would they have lost if Dr. Mercy Gabriel hadn't shown up? Was he the only one who wondered this?

He found himself moving toward this woman. He didn't want to know more about Dr. Mercy Gabriel. He didn't want to walk toward her, but she drew him. He offered her his hand to cover how confused he felt by his own reaction to her....

LYN COTE

and her husband, her real-life hero, became in-laws recently when their son married his true love. Lyn already loves her daughter-in-law and enjoys this new adventure in family stretching. Lyn and her husband still live on the lake in the north woods, where they watch a bald eagle and its young soar and swoop overhead throughout the year. She wishes the best to all her readers. You may email Lyn at l.cote@juno.com or write her at P.O. Box 864, Woodruff WI 54548. And drop by her blog, www.strongwomenbravestories.blogspot.com, to read stories of strong women in real life and in true-to-life fiction. "Every woman has a story. Share yours."

LYN COTE

Her Healing Ways

Steeple
Hill®

Published by Steeple Hill Books™

STEEPLE HILL BOOKS

Steeple
Hill®

Recycling programs
for this product may
not exist in your area.

ISBN-13: 978-0-373-82849-4

HER HEALING WAYS

www.SteepleHill.com

Printed in U.S.A.

There is no difference between Jews and Gentiles, between slaves and free men, between men and women; you are all one in union with Christ.
—*Galatians* 3:28

Also, if two lie down together, they will keep warm. But how can one keep warm alone?

Though one may be overpowered,
two can defend themselves.
—*Ecclesiastes* 4:11, 12

To Irene, Gail, Lenora, Patt, Carol, Kate, Val, Lois and Marty! Thanks for being my friends.

Chapter One

Idaho Territory, September 1868

High on the board seat, Mercy Gabriel sat beside the wagon master on the lead Conestoga. The line of the supply train slowed, pulling into the mining town Idaho Bend. Panicky-looking people ran toward it with bags and valises in hand. What was happening here? Like a cold, wet finger, alarm slid up Mercy's spine.

She reached down and urged her adopted daughter Indigo up onto the seat beside her, away from the onrushing people. Though almost sixteen now, Indigo shrank against Mercy, her darker face tight with concern. "Don't worry," Mercy whispered as confidently as she could.

She looked down at a forceful man who had pushed his way to the front. He was without a coat, his shirtsleeves rolled up and his colorfully embroidered vest buttoned askew. From the flamboyant vest, she guessed he must be a gambler. What would he want with them?

With one sweeping glance, he quelled the people shoving each other to get closer to the wagons. A commanding gambler. In her opinion, an unusual combination.

"Are there any medical supplies on this train?" he asked in a calm tone at odds with the mood of the people crowding around. "Two days ago, we telegraphed to Boise, asking for a doctor to come. But no one has. We've got cholera."

The dreaded word drenched the brave, brawny wagoners; they visibly shrank back from the man. It set off the crowd clamoring again.

Mercy's pulse raced. *No, not cholera.* Yet she hesitated only a second before revealing the truth about herself. Until this moment, she'd just been another traveler, not an object of mirth, puzzlement or derision. She braced herself for the inevitable reactions and rose. "I am a qualified physician."

Startled, the frantic crowd stopped pushing. As usual, every head swiveled, every face gawked at her.

"You?" the gambler challenged. "You're a woman."

Mercy swallowed a number of sardonic responses to this silly comment. She said, "I am a recent graduate of the Female Medical College of Pennsylvania. I also worked alongside Clara Barton as a nurse throughout the Civil War."

"You nursed in the war?" The gambler studied her, a quizzical expression on his face.

"Yes." Leaning forward, she held out her gloved hand. "I am Dr. Mercy Gabriel. And this is my assistant, Nurse Indigo."

He hesitated only a moment. Then, reaching up, he grasped her hand for a firm, brief handshake. "Beggars can't be choosers. I'm Lon Mackey. Will you come and help us?"

She wondered fleetingly why a gambler was taking charge here. She would have expected a mayor or—

Renewed commotion from the crowd, almost a mob now, grabbed her attention. People were trying to climb aboard the supply wagons. "Get us out of this town!" one of them shouted.

No, that would be disastrous! "Stop them," Mercy ordered, flinging up a hand. "No one from this town should be allowed to leave. They could infect everyone on the supply train and spread the disease to other towns."

At this, the wagoners rose and shouted, "Keep back! Quarantine! Quarantine!"

This only spurred the people of the mining town to try harder.

The head wagoner put out an arm, keeping Mercy and Indigo from getting down. "Wagoners, use your whips!"

The drivers raised their whips and snapped them expertly toward the mob. Mercy was horrified. Still muttering mutinously, the crowd fell back until safely out of range. Mercy swallowed her fear, her heart jumping.

"We will unload the shipment of supplies," the wagon master barked, "then we're leaving for the next town right away. And we're not taking on any new passengers."

People looked ready to make another charge toward the train, their expressions frantic, desperate.

"Thee must not give in to fear," Mercy declared. "There is hope. I am a qualified physician and my nurse is also trained." A silent Mercy stood very straight, knowing that her petite height of just over five feet didn't add much to her presence.

"You have nothing to fear, Dr. Gabriel," Lon Mackey announced, pulling a pistol from his vest. "I came to see if anyone could send us assistance. I didn't expect a doctor to be on the supply train. Please come. Lives are at stake."

Mercy moved to descend from the high buckboard. The wagon master let her go, shaking his head. Again he raised his whip as if ready to defend her. Barely able to breathe, Mercy descended, with Indigo in her wake. She addressed Lon Mackey. "I have medical supplies with me. Someone will need to get my trunk from the wagon."

"Get her trunk!" Lon ordered. "We need help. Thirteen people have already died in only three days."

The wagon master roared names, and another two

wagoners got down and started to unload Mercy's trunk, one cracking his whip to keep people back. The sullen mob still appeared ready to rush the wagons.

"No new passengers! Now back off or I start shooting!" The wagon master waved his pistol at the people about to surge forward. The sight of the gun caused a collective gasp. The mob fell back.

A wagoner pulled Mercy's bright red trunk, which was on casters, to her and Indigo. He touched the wide brim of his leather hat. "Good luck, ma'am."

Lon Mackey, also brandishing his pistol, led Mercy and Indigo through the crowd.

Indigo hovered closer to Mercy. They both knew what damage a bullet could do to flesh. And how a crowd could turn hostile. Mercy held tight to her slipping composure. *Father, no violence, please.*

Mercy called out a thanks and farewell to the gruff yet kind wagoners who had been their traveling companions for the past ten days on their way to Boise.

Lon Mackey led Mercy into the charcoal-gray twilight. She drew in the cool mountain air, praying for strength. The crowd milled around them, following, grumbling loudly, angrily.

Mercy tried to ignore them. She understood their fear but knew she must not get caught up in it. "Lon Mackey, has the town set up an infirmary?"

"We have concentrated the sick in the saloon. It was where the cholera started and it's the biggest building in town."

Mercy touched Lon's shoulder. "Cholera can snatch away life within a day. I'll do my best, as will my nurse-assistant. But people are going to die even after treatment. Cholera is a swift, mortal disease."

"That's why we got to get out of town, lady," one of the people in the surrounding crowd complained.

She looked at them. "Go to thy homes. If there has been anyone sick in thy house, open all the doors and windows and begin scrubbing everything—clothing, walls, floors, ceilings. Everything! Scrub with water as hot as thee can stand to use and with enough lye soap mixed into it to make thy eyes water. Use a scrub brush, not a cloth. That's thy only defense."

The crowd gawked at her.

"Now! Go!" Mercy waved her hands at them as if shooing away children. Several in the crowd turned and began to leave. The rest stared at her as if unable to move. "If thee acts quickly, thee and thy families may not succumb!"

This finally moved the people. They began running in several directions.

Lon Mackey started walking faster, waving for Indigo and Mercy to follow him. Mercy didn't complain about the brisk pace he set, but she had trouble keeping up. She forced herself on. People were dying.

The sun was sliding below the horizon of tall green mountains. How many evenings like this had she been faced with? People were dying. And she must help them. It was her calling and her privilege.

The gaudy front of the saloon loomed above the street, sticky with mud. Mercy and Indigo followed Lon Mackey inside, where another man was lighting the hanging oil lamps. Mercy gazed around and assessed the situation. Perhaps twenty people lay on blankets spread over the floor and the bar. Most were alone, but some were being ministered to by others, probably relatives.

Many of the patients' faces were bluish, the sign that cholera had already accomplished its pitiless, deadly work. The gorge rose in Mercy's throat. *Father, let my knowledge—as flimsy as it is—save some lives. Help me.*

Mercy took off her bonnet. "Good evening!" she announced in a loud, firm voice, though her stomach quivered like jelly. "I am Dr. Mercy Gabriel. I am a graduate of the Female Medical College of Pennsylvania. I nursed with Clara Barton throughout the war. I am here to see if I can save any of the sick. Now first—"

As she expected—dreaded—hoped to avoid, a sudden cacophony of voices roared in the previously quiet room.

"A woman doctor!"

"No!"

"Is this a joke?"

Mercy had heard this so many times before that it was hard not to shout back. A sudden wave of fatigue rolled over her. She resisted the urge to slump against the wall. As was common on most wagon trains she and Indigo had walked most of the ten days from the nearest railhead. She'd been looking forward to a hotel bed tonight. And now she must face the ridiculous but inevitable objections to her profession. The urge to stamp her foot at them nearly overwhelmed her good sense.

She endeavored to ignore the squawking about how she couldn't be a doctor. Who could trust a female doctor, they asked, and was that the best the gambler could do?

"Quiet." Lon Mackey's solid, male voice cut through the squabbling voices. He did not yell, he merely made himself heard over everyone else. The people fell silent. "What should we do to help you, Dr. Gabriel?"

In this chaotic and fearful room, Lon Mackey had asserted control. He was an impressive man. Mercy wondered what made him so commanding. She decided it wasn't his physical appearance as much as his natural self-assurance.

Mercy cleared her throat and raised her voice. There was no use sugarcoating the truth and doing so could only give false hope. "I am very sorry to say that those who have been sick for over twenty-four hours are without much hope. I need those cases to be moved to the far side of the room so that I can devote my energies to saving those who still have a chance to survive."

Again, the babble broke out.

Lon Mackey silenced all with a glance and the

lifting of one hand. "We don't have time to argue. You wanted help, I got a doctor—"

"But a woman—" someone objected.

He kept talking right over the objection. "The mayor's dead and no one else knew what to do. I went and got you a doctor, something I thought impossible." He propped his hands on his hips, looking dangerous to any opposition. "If Dr. Gabriel nursed in the war, she knows more than we do about taking care of sick people. If you don't want her to nurse your folks, then take them home. Anyone who stays will do what they're told by this lady doctor. Do you all understand that?"

Mercy was surprised to see the opposition to her melt away, even though Lon Mackey's pistol was back in his vest. She looked to the man again. She'd been distracted by his gambler's flashy vest. Now she noted that the shirt under it was of the finest quality, though smudged and wrinkled. Lon Mackey had once bought only the best.

He wasn't in his first youth, but he was also by no means near middle-aged. His face was rugged from the sun and perhaps the war—he had that look about him, the look of a soldier. And from just the little of him she'd seen in action, he was most probably an officer. He was used to giving orders and he expected to be obeyed. *And he is a man who cares about others.*

Mercy raised her voice and repeated, "I will set up my medical supplies near the bar. If thee isn't nursing a friend or loved one, I need thee to get buckets of hot water and begin swabbing down the floor area between patients.

"And get the word out that anyone who has any stomach cramps or nausea must come here immediately for treatment. If patients come in at the start of symptoms, I have a better chance of saving their lives. Now please, let's get busy. The cholera won't stop until we force it out."

The people stared at her.

She opened her mouth to urge them, but Lon Mackey barked, "Get moving! Now!"

And everyone began moving.

Lon mobilized the shifting of the patients and the scrubbing. And, according to the female doctor's instructions, a large pot was set up outside the swinging doors of the saloon to boil water for the cleaning.

He shook his head. A female doctor. What next? A tiny female physician who looked as if she should be dressed in ruffles and lace. He'd noted her Quaker speech and the plain gray bonnet and dress. Not your usual woman, by any means. And who was the young, pretty, Negro girl with skin the color of caramel? The doctor had said she was a trained nurse. How had that happened?

"Lon Mackey?"

He heard the Quaker woman calling his name and hurried to her. "What can I do for you, miss?"

"I want thee to ask someone to undertake a particular job. It has to be someone who is able to write, ask intelligent questions and think. I would do it myself, but I am about to begin saline infusions for these patients."

"What do you need done?"

"In order to end this outbreak, I need to know its source."

"Isn't it from the air?" Lon asked.

She smiled, looking pained. "I know the common wisdom is that this disease comes from the air. But I have done a great deal of study on cholera, and I believe that it comes from contaminated water or food. So I need to know the water source of each patient, alive or dead—if they shared some common food, if there was any group gathering where people might have drunk or ingested the same things. You said that the cholera appeared here in this saloon first. Is that correct?"

"Yes." He eyed her. *Contaminated water?* If there had been time, he would have liked to ask her about her research. But with people in agony and dying, there was no time for a long, scientific discussion. He rubbed the back of his neck and then rotated his head, trying to loosen the tight muscles.

"Was the person first taken with cholera living on these premises or just here to socialize?" she asked.

He grinned at her use of the ladylike word *socialize*. Most people would have used *carouse* or *sin* for stepping inside a saloon. This dainty woman continued to surprise him.

"It was the blacksmith. Comes in about twice a week for a beer or two. I think McCall was his name."

She nodded. "Has anyone at his home fallen ill?"

"Yes, his whole family is dead."

Her mouth tightened into a hard line. "That might indicate that his well was the culprit, but since the cholera seems to be more widespread…" She paused. "I need someone to question every patient about their water and food sources over the past week. And about any connection they might have had with the first victim." A loud, agonizing moan interrupted her.

"Will thee find someone," she continued, "to do that and write down the information so that I can go over it? This disease will continue to kill until we find its source and purify it. I assure you that the cholera epidemics that swept New York State in the 1830s were ended by cleaning up contaminated water sources."

He nodded. "I'll do it myself." From his inner vest pocket, he drew a small navy-blue notebook he always carried with him.

"I thank thee. Now I must begin the saline draughts. Indigo will try to make those suffering more comfortable." She turned to the bar behind her and lifted what he recognized as a syringe. He'd seen them in the war. The thought made him turn away in haste. *I will not think of syringes, men bleeding, men silent and cold...*

Several times during the long day, he glanced toward the bar and saw the woman kneeling and administering the saline solution by syringe to patient after patient. The hours passed slowly and painfully. How much good could salt water do? The girl, Indigo, was working her way through the seriously ill, speaking quietly, calming the distraught relatives.

He drew a long breath. He no longer prayed—the war had blasted any faith he'd had—but his spirit longed to be able to pray for divine help. Two more people died and were carried out, plunging them all into deeper gloom. He kept one eye on the mood of the fearful and excitable people in the saloon. A mob could form so easily. And now they had a target for blame. He wondered if the female doctor had thought of that.

Would this woman, armed with only saline injections and cleanliness, be able to save any lives? And if she didn't, what would the reaction be?

Much later that night, candles flickered in the dim, chilly room. When darkness had crept up outside the windows, voices had become subdued. Lon saw that for the first time in hours the Quaker was sitting down near the doors, sipping coffee and eating something. He walked up to her, drawn by the sight of her, the picture of serenity in the center of the cruel storm. Fatigue penetrated every part of his body. A few days ago he had been well-rested, well-fed and smiling. Then disaster had struck. That was how life treated them all. Until it sucked the breath from them and let them return to dust.

As he approached, she looked up and smiled. "Please wash thy hands in the clean water by the door, and I'll get thee a cup of fresh coffee."

Her smile washed away his gloom, making him do the impossible—he felt his mouth curving upward. She walked outside to where a fire had been burning all day to heat the boiled water for the cleaning and hand-washing. A large kettle of coffee had been kept brewing there, too. If he'd had any strength left, he would have objected. She wasn't here to wait on him. But it was easier to follow her orders and accept her kind offer. He washed his hands in the basin and then sank onto a wooden chair.

The Quaker walked with calm assurance through the swinging saloon doors as if she were a regular visitor of the place, as if they weren't surrounded by sick and dying people. She handed him a steaming cup of hot black coffee and a big ginger cookie. "I brought these cookies with me, so I know they are safe to eat."

It had been a long time since anyone had served him coffee without expecting to be paid. And the cookies reminded him of home, his long-gone home.

He pictured the broad front lawn. And then around the back, he imagined himself walking into the large kitchen where the white-aproned cook, Mary, was busy rolling out dough. But Mary had died while he was away at war, a sad twist. He shrugged his uncharacteristic nostalgia off, looking to the Quaker.

She sat across from him, sipping her coffee and nibbling an identical cookie. He gazed around him, smelling the harsh but clean odor of lye soap, which overpowered the less pleasant odors caused by the disease.

"You're lucky to have a maid who can also nurse the sick," he said. Ever since the unlikely pair had entered the saloon, the riddle of who the young black girl was had danced at the edge of his thoughts.

"Indigo is not my maid. She is my adopted daughter. I met her in the South during the war. She was only about seven at the time, an orphaned slave. Now she is nearly a woman and, as I said, a trained nurse."

He stared at her, blowing over his hot coffee to cool it. He'd never heard of a white person adopting a black child. He knew, of course, that Quakers had been at the forefront of abolitionism, far ahead of popular opinion. What did he think of this unusual adoption?

He shouldn't be surprised. Just like him, Dr. Mercy Gabriel obviously didn't live her life guided by what others might think. A woman who had nursed in the war. He recalled those few brave women who tirelessly nursed fallen soldiers, both blue and gray. As he sipped more bracing hot coffee, he studied this courageous woman's face. The resolve hardened within him. *I won't let any harm come to you, ma'am.*

"Will thee tell me if thee has found any connection between the first victim and the others?" she asked.

Glad for the distraction from his contemplation of her, Lon pulled the notebook out of his pocket and flipped through the pages. "The first victim, McCall, had just butchered and sold a few of his hogs to others in town. But some people who have died were not connected with this hog butchering or sale."

She nodded, still chewing the cookie. She daintily sipped her coffee and then said, "Once a contagion starts, others can be infected by coming into contact with those who have fallen ill."

"Are you certain it isn't due to an ill air blowing through town?" His large round cookie was sweet, spicy and chewy. He rested his head against the back of the chair.

She inhaled deeply. "Over a decade ago, Dr. John Snow in London did a study of the water supplies of victims of cholera in a poor district in London. The doctor was able to connect all the original cases to a pump in one neighborhood."

If Lon hadn't been so tired, he would have shown shock at this calm recitation of scientific information. This woman was interested in epidemics in London? Few men hereabouts would have been. He studied her more closely.

Her petite form had misled him initially, but

she was no bit of fluff. Despite death hovering in the room with them, her face was composed. She had taken off her bonnet to reveal pale, flaxen hair skimmed back into a tight bun, though some of the strands had managed to work themselves free. Her eyes—now, they stopped him. So blue—as blue as a perfect summer sky. Clear. Intelligent. Fearless.

He recalled her tireless work over the past hours, her calm orders and take-charge manner. Some men might resent it. He might have resented it once. But not here. Not now. Not in the face of such a wanton loss of lives. This woman might just be able to save people. Maybe even him.

"Do you think you're having any success here?" he asked in a lowered voice.

She looked momentarily worried. "I am doing my best, but my best will not save everyone who is stricken."

The swinging doors crashed open. A man holding a rifle burst into the saloon. "She's dying! I need the doctor!"

Chapter Two

Everyone around Lon and Mercy Gabriel froze.

"Did you hear me?" the man shrieked. "I was told a doctor's here! My wife's dying!"

Dr. Gabriel put down her cup, swallowing the last of her cookie. She rose and faced the man. "I am sorry to hear that. Why hasn't thee brought her here?"

"She won't come! She won't come into a saloon!" The man swung his rifle toward the Quaker. "You gotta come with me! Now! Save her!"

Lon leapt to his feet, pulling out his pistol, ready to shoot.

"Friend, I am heartily sorry for thee, but I cannot leave all these patients—" the woman motioned toward the crowded room "—to go to one. Thee must bring thy wife here."

"What?" The man gawked at her and raised his rifle to his eye to aim.

Lon moved toward the man slowly. He didn't want to shoot if he didn't have to.

"Thee must bring thy wife here. And then I will do whatever I can for her."

Lon marveled at the Quaker's calm voice. It shouldn't have surprised him that the man with the rifle was also confounded. The man froze, staring forward.

Dr. Gabriel moved away to a patient and began to give the woman another dose of the saline infusion.

"You have to come with me, lady!" the man demanded. "My wife won't come here."

Dr. Gabriel glanced over her shoulder. "Is she still conscious?"

The man lowered his rifle. "No."

"Well, then what is stopping thee from carrying her here? If she is unconscious or delirious, she won't know where she is." The Quaker said this in the same reasonable tone, without a trace of fear. Lon had rarely heard the like.

This woman was either crazy or as cool as they came.

The man swung the gun above Mercy's head and fired, shattering one of the bulbous oil lamps behind the bar.

Lon lunged forward and struck the man's head with the butt of his pistol, wrestling the rifle from him. The man dropped to the floor.

"Does he have a fever?" the Quaker asked as she gazed at the fallen man.

Lon gawked at her. Unbelieving. Astounded.

"Does he have a fever?" she prompted.

After stooping to check, Lon nodded. "Yes, he's fevered. Doctor, *you* are very cool under fire."

She gazed at him, still unruffled. "Unfortunately, this is not the first time a weapon has been aimed at me." She turned away but said over her shoulder, "Set him on the floor on a blanket. Then please find out where this poor man's wife is and see if she's alive. I doubt there is anything I can do for her. But we must try. And, Lon Mackey, will thee please keep asking questions? We must get to the source before more people die."

Lon carried the unconscious man and laid him down, then asked another person where the man's home was. As he turned to leave, he snatched up the rifle and took it with him. He didn't want anybody else waving it around.

Since the war, nothing much surprised him. But Dr. Mercy Gabriel had gotten his attention. *She could have gotten herself killed. And she didn't even so much as blink.*

Mercy went about her round of injections, thinking of Lon and the ease with which he'd subdued the distraught man. She had never gotten used to guns, yet this was the second time today men had been forced to draw guns to protect her.

A young woman with a little girl in her arms rushed through the swinging doors. "My child! My Missy is having cramping. They said that cramping…" The woman's face crumpled and she visibly fought for control. "Please save her. She's only four. Please." The woman held out her daughter to Mercy.

"Just cramps, nothing else?"

"Just cramps. She started holding her stomach and crying about a half hour ago." Tears poured down the woman's face.

"Thee did exactly right in bringing her here so quickly. I will do what I can." Mercy lifted the child from her mother's trembling arms, tenderly laid the little girl on the bar and smiled down at her. "Thee must not be afraid. I know what to do."

Mercy felt the child's forehead. Her temperature was already rising. Mercy fought to keep her focus and not give in to worry and despair. God was in this room, not just the deadly cholera.

The mother hovered nearby, wringing her hands.

Mercy bent to listen to the child's heart with her stethoscope. "Missy, I need thee to sit up and cough for me."

The mother began to weep. Mercy glanced at Indigo, who nodded and drew the woman outside. Then Mercy went about examining the child. Soon she glanced over and saw that Indigo had left the woman near the doors and was continuing her rounds of the patients. Indigo bathed their reddened faces with water and alcohol, trying to fight their fevers.

Mercy listened to the little girl's abdomen and heard the telltale rumbling. No doubt the child had become infected. Mercy closed her eyes for one second, sending a prayer heavenward. *Father, help me save this little life.*

A call for help came from the far side of the room. Mercy looked over and her spirits dropped. One of the patients was showing signs of the mortal end of this dreaded disease. A woman—no doubt the wife of the dying man—rose and shouted for help again.

Mercy watched Indigo weave swiftly between the pallets on the wood floor to reach the woman's side. Mercy looked away. She hated early death, needless death, heartless death. Her usual composure nearly slipped. As the woman's sobbing filled the room, Mercy tightened her control. *I cannot give in to emotion. I must do what I can to save this child. Father, keep me focused.*

Mercy mixed the first dose of the herbal medication her mother had taught her to concoct, which was better than any patented medicine she'd tried. "Now, Missy, thee must drink this in order to get better."

"I want my mama." The little girl's face wrinkled up in fear. "Mama. Mama."

Mercy picked up the child and cradled her in her arms. "Thy mama's right beside the door, see?" Mercy turned so the child could glimpse her mother. "She wants me to make thee better. Now this will taste a little funny, but not that bad. I've taken it many times. Now here, take a sip, Missy. Just a little sip, sweet child."

Missy stared into Mercy's eyes. Then she opened her mouth and began to sip the chalky medicine. She wrinkled her nose at the taste but kept on sipping until the small cup was empty.

"Excellent, Missy. Thee is a very good girl. Now I'm going to lay thee down again, and thy mama will come and sit with thee. I will be giving thee more medicine soon."

"It tasted funny."

"I know but thee drank it all, brave girl."

About half an hour later, Mercy was kneeling beside the man who had burst into the saloon and was still unconscious. She carefully gave him a dose of saline water. It seemed a pitiful medicine to combat such a deadly contagion. But it was the only thing she knew of that actually did something to counteract cholera's disastrous effect on the human body. And no one even knew why. *There's so much that I wish I knew—that I wish someone knew.*

It was nearly dawn when she heard her name and glanced up to see Lon Mackey. "Did thee find this man's wife?"

His face sank into grimmer lines. "She's dead."

The news twisted inside Mercy. She shook her head over the loss of another life. Then she motioned for him to lean closer to her. She whispered, "We

must find the source or this disease will kill at least
half in this community."

The stark words sank like rocks from her stomach to her toes. She forced herself to go on. "That
is the usual death rate for unchecked cholera. Has
thee found out *anything* that gives us a hint of the
source?"

"I've talked to everyone. The little girl's mother
told me something I've heard from several of the
others."

"What is that?" Mercy asked, turning to concentrate on slowly infusing saline into the man's vein.

"Wild blackberry juice was served at the church
a week ago Sunday. There was a reception for the
children's Sunday-school recitation," he murmured.

Mercy looked up into his face. "Wild blackberry
juice? Who made it?"

"It was a concoction Mrs. McCall made from
crushed berries, their good well water and sugar.
Mrs. McCall was the wife of the first victim. And
the whole of his family was ailing first and all
succumbed."

Mercy sat back on her heels. Closing her eyes,
she drew in a slow breath, trying to calm her racing
heart. Lon Mackey may have found her the answer.
"That tells me what I need to know. Thee must do
exactly as I say. Will thee?"

Hours ago Lon wouldn't have done anything a
female stranger told him to do. But he would do

whatever Mercy Gabriel asked. He just hoped it would work—passions were running high outside the saloon. "What must I do?"

"Go to the McCall house and examine the water source. Examine the house and the grounds with great care. Take a healthy man with thee as a witness."

"What am I looking for?" he asked, leaning closer. The faint fragrance of lavender momentarily distracted him from her words.

"After the 1834 cholera epidemic, New York State passed laws forbidding the discarding of animal carcasses in or near any body of water. Does that help thee?" she asked.

Without a word of doubt, Lon rose and strode outside. He motioned to the bartender, Tom Banks, who was adding wood to the fire under the kettle of water the Quaker required to be kept boiling. "We've got a lead on what might have caused the cholera. Come with me. She told me what to look for and where," Lon said.

The two of them hurried down the empty street. Dawn was breaking and normally people would be stirring, stepping outside. But every shop in town was closed up tight and all the houses were eerily quiet. No children had played outside for days now. Even the stray dogs lying in the alleys looked bewildered.

"Do you think this Quaker woman, this *female* doctor, knows what she's doing?" the bartender asked.

Lon shrugged. "Proof's in the pudding," he said.

But if he had to wager, his money would be on Mercy Gabriel.

At the McCalls, the two of them walked around the empty house to the well. He was used to violent death and destruction but the unnatural silence and creeping dread of cholera was getting to him. Everything was so still.

"The Quaker told me to examine the well and any other water source."

"Doesn't she know that contagions come from bad air?" Tom objected.

"She knows more than we do," Lon replied. "Every time I talk to her, I know more about this scourge than I did before." Of course, that didn't mean she could save everyone. In times like these, however, he'd found that a show of assurance could avert the worst of hysteria. He didn't want anyone else bursting into the saloon and letting loose with a rifle.

The two of them approached the well. It was a primitive affair with the pump sitting on a rough wooden platform.

"I don't know what we'll find that's not right," Tom grumbled. "From what I heard, the McCalls always had sweet water. That's why they always brought the juice."

Lon stared down at the wooden platform. Part of it was warping and lifting up. "Let's find a crowbar or hammer." They went to the barn and found both. Soon they were prying up the boards over the McCalls' well.

Both of them cursed when they saw what was floating in the water.

They cleaned out the well and then pumped water for a good half hour. Then they capped the well cover down as tight as they could. Tom and Lon walked silently back to the saloon. Lon hit the swinging door first and with great force, his anger at the senseless loss of life fueling a furious fire within. The two swinging panels cracked against the wall. Every head turned.

Lon crossed to the Quaker doctor. "We found dead rats floating in the McCalls' well."

The Quaker rose to face him, looking suddenly hopeful. "That would do it. Had the well cover become compromised?"

"It was warped and loose."

She sighed and closed her eyes. "We need to find out if everyone who is ill has been brought here. Anyone who drank the juice or who came in contact with a person falling ill from it should be checked. Then we need to make sure that every house where the illness has presented is scrubbed completely with hot water with a high concentration of lye soap."

"That will end this?" Lon studied her earnest face, hoping against hope that she would say yes.

"If we kill off all the bacteria that carry the disease, the disease will stop infecting people. The bacteria most likely move from surface to surface. I believe that in order to become ill, a person must ingest the contaminated water or come into contact with something an infected person has touched. Does thee need anything more from me to proceed?"

"No, you've made yourself quite clear."

She smiled at him. "Thee is an unusual man, Lon Mackey."

He couldn't help but smile back, thinking that she was unusual herself. He hoped she was right about the cause of the cholera. Only time would tell.

The last victim of the cholera epidemic died seven days after Mercy and Indigo came to town. When people had begun recovering and going home, the few remaining sick had been moved to one of the small churches in town after it had been scrubbed mercilessly clean. And the vacated saloon was dealt with in the same way. The towns-people doing the cleaning complained about the work, but they did it.

Eight days after getting off the wagon train, Mercy stood in the church doorway. She gazed out at the sunny day, her body aching with fatigue. She had slept only a few hours each day for the past week, and her mind and body didn't appreciate that treatment. Only three patients lingered, lying on pallets around the church pulpit.

The new mayor came striding up the path to the church. "The saloon is clean and back in business."

She gazed at him. Even though she was glad there was no longer a need for a large hospital area, did he expect her to say that the saloon being back in business was a good thing?

"I took up a collection from the people you helped." He drew out an envelope and handed it to her. "When do you think you'll be leaving town?"

Mercy made him wait for her answer. She opened the envelope and counted out four dollars and thirty-five cents. *Four dollars and thirty-five cents for saving half the lives in this town of over a thousand.* She wasn't surprised at this paltry amount. After all, she was a female doctor, not a "real" doctor.

Mercy stared into the man's eyes. "I have no plans to leave." She had thought of going on to Boise, but then had decided to stay where she had shown that she knew something about doctoring. Many would discount her efforts to end the epidemic, but others wouldn't—she hoped. "And, friend, if this town doesn't want a recurrence of cholera, thee should have all the people inspect their wells and streams."

The mayor made a harrumphing sound. "We're grateful for the nursing you've done, but we still believe what real doctors believe. The cholera came from a bad wind a few weeks ago."

Mercy didn't bother to take offense. *There are none so blind as those who will not see.* "I am not the only doctor who believes that cholera comes from contaminated water. And thee saw thyself that the McCalls' well was polluted. Would thee drink water with a dead rat in it?"

The mayor made the same harrumphing sound

and ignored her question. "Again, ma'am, you have our gratitude." He held out his hand.

Mercy shook it and watched him walk away.

"The thankless wretch."

She turned toward the familiar voice. Lon Mackey lounged against the corner of the small white clapboard church. He looked different than the first time they'd met. His clothing was laundered and freshly pressed, and his colorful vest was buttoned correctly. He was a handsome man. She chuckled at his comment.

"It is so predictable." She drew in a long breath. "I've heard it all before. 'You're just a woman. What could you possibly know?' Over and over."

"Why do you put up with it?"

She chuckled again.

The sound irritated Lon. "I don't know what's funny about this. You should be taken seriously. How much did the town pay you?"

Mercy sighed, handing him the envelope. "Human nature is what's funny. Even when confronted by the truth about the cause of the epidemic, the average male and most females refuse to believe a woman would know more than a man would."

They'd paid her less than five dollars. He voiced his disgust by saying, "But your idea about the cause of cholera is based on what male doctors have discovered, isn't it?"

She nodded, tucking the envelope into the small leather purse in her skirt pocket. "But I could have gotten it wrong. I am, after all, just a poor, inferior, weak female who must always defer to men who *always* know better than women do."

Her words grated against his nerves like sandpaper on sensitive skin. Why? Was he guilty of thinking this, too? He found himself moving toward this woman. He shut his mouth. He didn't want to know more about Dr. Mercy Gabriel. He didn't want to walk toward her, but she drew him. He offered her his hand to cover how disgruntled and confused he felt by his reaction to her.

She smiled and shook it. "I thank thee, Lon Mackey. Thee didn't balk very much at following a woman's directions."

He didn't know what to say to this. Was she teasing him or scolding him? Or being genuine? He merely smiled and turned away. The saloon was open again and he had to win some money to pay for his keep. He would be staying in the saloon almost round the clock for the next few days—he'd seen the men of the town coming back full force. How had he come this far from the life he'd been born to? The answer was the war, of course.

He walked toward the saloon, hearing voices there louder and rowdier than usual. No doubt watching the wagons carrying people to the cemetery made men want to forget the harsh realities of life with lively conversation and laughter. Nearly seventy people had succumbed to cholera. How many would they have lost if Dr. Mercy Gabriel hadn't shown up? Was he the only one who wondered this?

And why wouldn't the Quaker woman leave his mind?

Images of Mercy over the past few hectic days popped into his mind over and over again. Mercy kneeling beside a patient and then rising to go to the next, often with a loud, burdened sigh. Mercy speaking softly to a weeping relative. Mercy staggering to a chair and closing her eyes for a short nap and then rising again. He passed a hand over his forehead as if he could wipe away the past week, banish Mercy Gabriel from his mind. But she wasn't the kind of woman a man could forget easily. *But I must.*

Chapter Three

The morning after the final patient had recovered, Mercy decided it was time to find both a place to live and a place to start her medical practice. She wondered if she should ask Lon Mackey for help.

As she stood looking down the main street of the town, Indigo said, "Aunt Mercy?"

Mercy looked into Indigo's large brown eyes. Indigo had always called her Aunt Mercy—the title of "mother" had never seemed right to either of them. "Yes?"

"Are we going to stand here all day?" Indigo grinned.

Mercy leaned her head to the side. "I'm sorry. I was lost in thought." She didn't reveal that the thoughts had been about Lon Mackey. He had vanished several days ago, returning to the largest saloon on the town's one muddy street. His abrupt departure from their daily life left her hollow, blank, somehow weakened.

Indigo nodded as if she had understood both Mercy's thoughts and gaze.

Mercy drew in a deep breath and hoped it would revive her. This was the place she had been called to. Only time would reveal if it would become home. "Let's pull the trunk along. There must be some rooming houses in a town this size." The two of them moved to the drier edge of the muddy track through town.

Mercy's heart stuttered as she contemplated once again facing a town unsympathetic to a female doctor and a black nurse. Lon Mackey's withdrawal from her sphere also blunted her mood. As she strode up the unpaved street, she tried to center herself, calm herself. *God is a very present help in time of trouble. Lon Mackey helped me and accepted me for what I am—there will surely be others, won't there?*

A large greenwood building with big hand-painted letters announcing "General Store" loomed before her. Mercy left the trunk on the street with Indigo and entered. Her heart was now skipping beats.

"Good day!" she greeted a man wearing a white apron standing behind the rough wood-slab counter. "I'm new in town and looking for lodging. Can thee recommend a boardinghouse here?"

The man squinted at her. "You're that female doctor, aren't you?"

Mercy offered her hand. "Yes, I am Dr. Mercy Gabriel. And I'm ready to set up practice here."

He didn't take her hand.

She cleared her throat, which was tightening under his intense scrutiny.

"I'm Jacob Tarver, proprietor. I never met a female doctor before. But I hear you helped out nursing the cholera patients."

"I doctored the patients as a qualified physician," Mercy replied, masking her irritation. Then she had to suffer through the usual catechism of how she'd become a doctor, along with the usual response that no one would go to a female doctor except maybe for midwifing. She could have spoken both parts and he could have remained silent. People were so predictable in their prejudices.

Finally, she was able to go back to her question about lodging. "Where does thee suggest we find lodging, Jacob Tarver?"

He gave her an unhappy look. "That girl out there with you?"

Mercy had also been ready for this. Again, she kept her bubbling irritation hidden. If one chose to walk a path much different than the average, then one must put up with this sort of aggravation—even when one's spirit rebelled against it. "Yes, Indigo is my adopted daughter and my trained nursing assistant."

The proprietor looked at her as if she'd lost her mind but replied, "I don't know if she'll take you in, but go on down the street to Ma Bailey's. She might have space for you in her place."

Mercy nodded and thanked him. Outside, she motioned to Indigo and off they went to Ma Bailey's. Mercy's feet felt like blocks of wood. A peculiar kind of gloom was beginning to take hold of her. She saw the boardinghouse sign not too far down the street, but the walk seemed long. Once again, Mercy knocked on the door, leaving Indigo waiting with the red trunk.

A buxom woman in a faded brown dress and a soiled apron opened the door. "I'm Ma Bailey. What can I do for you?"

Feeling vulnerable, Mercy prayed God would soften this woman's heart. "We're looking for a place to board."

The interrogation began and ended as usual with Ma Bailey saying, "I don't take in people who ain't white, and I don't think doctorin' is a job for womenfolk."

Mercy's patience slipped, a spark igniting. "Then why is it the mother who always tends to sick children and not the father?"

"Well, that's different," Ma Bailey retorted. "A woman's supposed to take care of her own."

"Well, I'm different. I want to take care of more than my daughter. If God gave me the gift of healing, who are thee to tell me that I don't have it?"

"Your daughter?" The woman frowned.

Mercy glanced over her shoulder. "I adopted Indigo when she was—"

"Don't hold with that, neither."

"I'm sorry I imposed on thy time," Mercy said and walked away. She tried to draw up her reserves, to harden herself against the expected unwelcome here. No doubt many would sit in judgment upon her today. But she had to find someone who would take them in. Lon Mackey came into her thoughts again. Could she ask the man for more help? Who else could put in a good word for them?

Heavenly Father, plead my case. For the very first time, she wondered if heaven wasn't listening to her here.

Midafternoon Lon took a break from the poker table. He stepped outside and inhaled the cool, damp air of autumn. He found himself scanning the street and realized he was looking for *her.* He literally shook himself. The Quaker was no longer his business.

Then he glimpsed Indigo across the mud track, sitting on the red trunk. As he watched, the female doctor came out of a rough building and spoke to Indigo. Then the two of them went to the next establishment. Dr. Gabriel knocked and went inside. Within minutes, she came back outside and she and the girl headed farther down the street to the next building. What was she doing? Introducing herself? Or trying to get a place to stay? That sobered Lon. No one was going to rent a room to a woman of color. Lon tried to stop worrying and caring about what happened to this unusual pair. *This can't be the first time the good doctor has faced this. And it's not my job to smooth the way for them. In fact, it would be best if they moved on to a larger city.*

He turned back inside, irritated with himself for having this inner debate. The saloon was now empty, sleepy. Since his nighttime schedule didn't fit with regular boardinghouses, he'd rented a pallet in the back of the saloon. He went there now to check on his battered leather valise. He'd locked it and then chained it to the railing that went upstairs, where the saloon girls lived. He didn't have much in the valise but his clothing and a few mementoes. Still, it was his. He didn't want to lose it.

Mentally, he went through the few items from his past that he'd packed: miniature portraits of his late parents, his last letter from them as he fought in Virginia and the engagement ring Janette had returned to him. This last article wasn't a treasured token but a reminder of how rare true love was in this world. He wondered if Mercy Gabriel had ever taken a chance on falling in love.

That thought ended his musing. Back to reality. He'd have to play some very good poker tonight and build up his funds again. He lay down on his pallet for a brief nap. The night was probably going to be a long, loud one.

* * *

Mercy faced cold defeat. She had been turned away at every boardinghouse door and had been told at the hotels that they had no vacancies. She sensed the reason was because of Indigo's skin color, a painful, razor-sharp thought. A cold rain now drizzled, chilling her bone-deep. She and Indigo moved under the scant cover of a knot of oak and elm trees.

"Well, Aunt Mercy, this wouldn't be the first time we've slept under the stars," Indigo commented, putting the unpleasant truth into words.

Mercy drew in a long breath. She didn't want to reply that those days had been when they were both younger and the war was raging. Mercy had found little Indigo shivering beside the road, begging. Mercy had turned thirty-one this January. The prospect of sleeping out at twenty-one had felt much different than sleeping without cover nearly a decade later. Both she and Indigo sat down on the top of their trunk. *Father, we need help. Soon. Now.* Then defeat swallowed her whole.

The acrid smoke from cigars floated above the poker table. Lon held his cards close to his chest just in case someone was peeking over his shoulder for an accomplice, cheating at the table. So far he hadn't been able to play for more than chicken stakes. Piano music and bursts of laughter added to the noisy atmosphere. He was holding a flush—not the best hand, but not the worst, either. Could he bluff the others into folding?

"You got to know that strange female?" the man across from him asked as he tossed two more coins into the ante pile. The man was dressed a bit better than the other miners and lumberjacks in the saloon. He had bright red hair and the freckled complexion to match. Lon thought he'd said his name was Hobson.

Lon made an unencouraging sound, hoping to change the topic of conversation. He met the man's bid and raised it. The coin clinked as it hit the others.

"You know anything about her?" Hobson asked.

Lon nodded, watching the next player, a tall, lean man called Slattery, with a shock of gray at one temple. He put down two cards and was dealt two more.

"You know anything about her? I mean, can she really doctor?" redheaded Hobson asked again.

"She's a doc all right," Lon conceded. "I saw her certificate myself. She showed it to me the second night she was in town. It's in her black bag."

"We need a doc here," Hobson said as the last of the four players made his final bet of the game.

"Don't need no woman doctor," Slattery replied. "She's unnatural. A woman like that."

Lon started a slow burn. Images of Mercy Gabriel caring for the cholera victims spun through his mind. "She's a Quaker. They think different, talk different."

The other player, a small man with a mustache, grunted. "Forget the woman doctor. Play cards."

"She's honest and goodhearted." Lon heard these words flow from his mouth, unable to stop them.

"I don't hold with Quakers' odd ways," Slattery said.

Hobson glared at Slattery as he laid down his cards. "My grandparents were Quakers. You could look your whole life and not find finer people. So what if they say 'thee' and 'thy'? It's a free country."

As Lon laid down his own hand, he sighed. His flush beat every other hand on the table. A tight place within him eased—winning was good. He scooped up the money in the ante pile.

"Well, nobody would take them in," Slattery said, looking irritated at losing but satisfied to be able to say something slighting about Dr. Gabriel. "She has a black girl with her. Tells everyone she adopted her. If nobody takes them in, they'll have to go elsewhere. And good riddance, I say." Slattery shoved away from the table and headed toward the bar.

Hobson looked after him and turned to Lon. "We need a doctor in this place. Logging and mining can be dangerous. Anybody see where those two women went?"

"When I came in, they were wrapped in blankets, sitting on the trunk under that clump of oaks at the end of the street," Lon said.

Hobson stood up and headed toward the door.

The quiet man with the mustache looked to Lon. "Let's find a couple more—"

Two other men came and slid into the seats left vacant by Hobson and Slattery. Out of the corner of his eye, Lon glimpsed Hobson leaving.

Lon hoped Digger was going to help out the two stubborn women. He didn't like to see anyone homeless, but they had chosen a path that put them at odds with popular sentiment. In any event, how could he provide them with a place to stay? Would they want to bunk in the back of the saloon, as he did? Of course not. With regret, he turned his mind to his new competitors.

Mercy shivered as the night began to fold them into its cool, damp arms. She and Indigo had wrapped themselves in their blankets and perched on top of the trunk, which was wedged between two trees so it wouldn't move. Oil lamps and candles shone in the dwellings so they weren't sitting in complete darkness. Mercy kept her eyes on those lights, kept praying that someone would offer them a place, someone would come out—

A man was striding down the street in their direction. Was he headed past them for home? She heard him coming, splashing in the shallow puddles. A lantern at his hip glimmered.

"He's heading straight toward us," Indigo whispered.

Mercy caught the fear in Indigo's voice, and it trembled through her. Was violence to be added to insult here? She leaned against Indigo, her voice quavering. "Don't be afraid. No one is going to harm us."

"You that woman doctor?" the man asked in a brisk tone, his copper hair catching the lantern light.

"Yes, I am." Mercy didn't know whether she should stand, or even if she could.

"You two can't sleep out here all night. Follow me." The man turned and began striding away.

His unforeseen invitation sent her thoughts sprawling. "Please, friend, where is thee going?"

He turned back and halted. "I'm Digger Hobson, the manager of one of the mining outfits hereabouts. I'm going to take you to the mining office for the night."

She didn't want to turn the man down, but how would they sleep there? Her nerve was tender, but she managed to ask, "Mining office?"

"Yeah, I bunked there till I got a place of my own. Now come on. Let's not waste time." The man strode away from them.

With a tiny yelp, Indigo jumped off the trunk, swirled her blanket higher so it wouldn't drag in the mud, and began hauling the trunk behind her.

Coming out of her shock, Mercy followed Indigo's example and grabbed the valises, hurrying on stiff legs through the mud. The two of them caught up with Hobson where he had stopped. The building had a hand-painted sign that read "Acme Mining Office."

"Come on in. It's not much, but it's better than sleeping out under the trees all night. I can't understand why no one would take you in."

Mercy could only agree with him. But she was so unnerved she didn't trust herself yet to speak.

"Some people don't like me because of my color," Indigo said, surprising Mercy. Mercy hadn't mentioned the rude comments people had made about Indigo. But since none of them had kept their voices down, Indigo had probably overheard them. The area around Mercy's heart clenched.

"I fought in the war to set you free," Digger said. "Some folks think you all ought to go back to Africa. But I don't think I'd like to go there myself."

"Not me, either, sir. I'm an American," Indigo stated.

"Thee is very kind, Digger Hobson." Mercy found her voice. She wondered why this welcome hospitality still left her emotionless inside. Perhaps rejection was more powerful than kindness. But that shouldn't be.

"We need a doctor here. I wouldn't have asked for a female doctor, but if you really got a certificate and everything, then we'll make do with you. Mining can be a rough trade."

Mercy tried to sort through these words but the unusual numbness she hoped was due to the chill and fatigue caused her only to nod. Certificate? Who knew she had a certificate?

Her dazed mind brought up a scene from the saloon infirmary. Lon had been looking over her shoulder as she had dug into the bottom of her black bag. She'd taken out her framed certificate so she could search better.

So Lon had been talking about her? What had he said?

"Dr. Gabriel is tired," Indigo said. "Where are the beds?"

Mercy realized that she had just been standing there, not paying attention to this kind man.

"There are two cots in the back room. I'm going farther up the mountain now, to get to bed. Have a busy day tomorrow." As he spoke, he led them through an office area into a back room where there was a potbellied stove and two bare cots.

"Do you have bedding with you?" he asked.

"Yes, yes, thank you," Indigo stammered.

As Hobson turned to leave, he lit a tall candle on the stove. "Good night, ladies." He handed Mercy the key. "Lock up behind me. Two women alone can't be too careful."

When Mercy did not move, Indigo took the key and followed him back through the office. Mercy waited, frozen in place, watching the flickering, mesmerizing candle flame. She had heard of people falling asleep standing up. Was that happening to her?

Indigo entered, helped Mercy off with her blanket and steered her into a wooden chair beside the stove. "You sit here, Aunt Mercy. You look really tired."

Mercy sat, the numbness still clutching her. This was more than the usual fatigue, Mercy sensed. Indigo began humming "Be Thou My Vision" as she opened the trunk, got out their wrinkled sheets and pillows, and made up the two cots. "God has provided for us again."

Mercy wanted to agree. But her tongue lay at the bottom of her mouth, limp and wayward. Then Indigo was there in front of her, kneeling to unbutton her shoes. "You're just very tired, that's all. I think you need a few days of rest and good food. And you'll be right as a good spring rain."

Indigo led Mercy over to the cot nearest the stove. "I think I'll make up a small fire and brew a cup of tea for both of us. Then we'll go to bed and let the fire die down on its own. It's not that cold, not as cold as it can be in Pennsylvania in late September."

Indigo kept up small talk as she cared for them both. Mercy let herself sit and listen. She could do nothing more. She was tired, not just from the cholera epidemic or walking behind the wagons to get here. She was tired to the marrow of her bones from the unkind way people treated each other.

The mayor's insults the other day, diminishing her role in stopping the epidemic which could have killed him. The unfriendly and judgmental way people had looked at them today as they walked down Main Street. And Lon Mackey, who she'd begun to consider an ally, disappearing from her life when she most needed help. These had leeched the life from her.

In this whole town, they had encountered one kind man out of how many? The others, when they had ample room to take them in, would have let her and Indigo sleep outside. Well, she shouldn't be surprised. There had been no room at the inn for Mary and Joseph. And baby Jesus had been born among the cattle. Lon Mackey's face came to mind clearly. She had been hoping he would come to their aid, clearly. Foolish beyond measure. She sighed and closed her eyes. Whatever connection she had felt with him had been an illusion. Something inside her flickered and then went out, extinguished.

Despite his best efforts, Lon woke while it was still morning. Dr. Gabriel's face flashed before his eyes. He rolled over. Around four o'clock in the morning, when the saloon had finally shut its doors, he'd been unable to keep himself from going out with a lantern and checking to see if the two women were still sitting under the tree. This concern for their welfare could only spring from the life-threatening circumstances under which they'd met and nothing else, he insisted silently.

When he'd found, in the early morning light, that they were no longer under the tree, he'd been able to go to his bed and sleep. He would let the God they believed in take care of them from now on.

Though it was much earlier than he ever cared to be awake, he found he could not go back to sleep.

He sat up, disgusted with himself. After shaving and donning his last fresh collar, he strode out into the thin sunshine to find breakfast. The town was bustling. He stood looking up and down the street. Then drawn by the mingled fragrances of coffee, bacon and biscuits, he headed for breakfast at a café on the nearest corner.

On the way, he saw Dr. Gabriel step outside a mining office and begin sweeping the wooden platform in front of the place. Something deep inside nudged him to avoid her, but he couldn't be that rude. Tipping his hat, he said, "Good morning, Dr. Gabriel."

"Lon Mackey, good morning."

"Is this where you stayed last night?" he asked.

"Yes," she replied. "A man, Digger Hobson, let us stay. I'm just tidying up a bit to thank him for his kindness."

"I'm glad to hear you found a place. Yesterday, I saw you going door to door…" He caught himself before he said more.

"It is always difficult for Indigo and me in a new place." She also paused and gazed into his eyes.

He glanced away. "You still think you can establish yourself here?"

"I do. I hope…" Her voice faded.

He denied the urge to try to talk sense into her. Still, he lingered. This woman had earned his regard. And the feeling of working together to fight the cholera had taken him back to his previous life when he'd had a future. He broke away from her effect on him. "I'll bid you good day then."

Mercy wanted to stop him, speak to him longer. But even as she opened her mouth, she knew she must not. Their paths should not cross again except in this casual way. Why did that trouble her? Just because she had found him so easy to work with meant nothing to her day-to-day life. She went on sweeping, quelling the sudden, surprising urge to cry. Lon had believed in her abilities and trusted her in a way that few other men ever had, and it was hard to simply let that go.

At the sound of footsteps on the office's wooden floor, she turned to greet Indigo. "Thee slept well?"

"Yes. I feel guilty for lying in so long. You know I never sleep late."

"I think thee needed the extra rest." She watched as Lon Mackey walked into the café on the corner. She had no appetite, which was unusual, but the two of them must eat to keep up their strength. "Indigo, would thee go down to the café, buy us breakfast and bring it back here?"

Indigo's stomach growled audibly in response. The girl grinned. "Why don't we just go there and eat?"

Because he's there. "I'm not in the mood for company this morning." That wasn't a lie, unfortunately. Mercy pulled her purse out of her pocket and gave it to Indigo. She gave Mercy a penetrating look, then left, singing quietly to herself.

Mercy walked inside the office and looked out the smudged front window. She thought of going around town again this afternoon, trying to get to know all the residents, trying to begin to soften their resistance, to change their minds about a woman doctor. But the thought of stepping outside again brought her near to tears.

For the first time she could recall, she had no desire to go out into the sunshine. No desire to go on doing what she must in order to change opinions about her. To carry out her mission. This sudden absence of purpose was alien to her.

The fact was she didn't want to talk to or see anyone save Indigo. Or, truth be told, Lon Mackey. Though she'd been hurt that he hadn't come to her aid, the fact that he'd gone looking for her in the early morning had lifted her heart some. She wrapped her arms around herself and shivered in spite of the lingering warmth from the potbellied stove.

She went over in her mind the brief conversation with Lon about his concern and about his opposition to her way of life. What they had said to each other wasn't as telling as what they hadn't said. She couldn't have imagined the strong connection they'd forged, and she couldn't believe it had ended when the cholera had.

Something was shifting inside her. And she was afraid to venture toward its cause.

* * *

A week had passed. Friday was payday and the saloon was standing room only. The poker table was ringed with a few farmers, but mostly miners and lumberjacks watched the game in progress. In the back of Lon's mind, the fact that he hadn't seen Dr. Gabriel on the street since she'd moved into the mining office niggled at him. Had she fallen sick? Should he go check on her?

He brushed the thought away like an aggravating fly. He'd done much this week to rebuild his reserves. And tonight's game was not for chicken stakes. Nearly a hundred dollars in gold, silver and bills had been tossed into the ante. If Lon lost this game, he'd be broke again.

His three competitors included the same small, mustached man whom Lon had gambled with every night the past week. The other two were a tall, slender young man and a dark-haired miner. The young half breed spoke with a French accent. Perhaps he was a mix of Métis, Indian and French. Either way, Lon pegged him as a young buck out to have all the fun he could, no doubt with the first good money he'd ever earned. The miner looked ill-tempered, old enough to know better than to cause trouble. But wise enough? Time would tell.

Lon stared at his cards—just a pair of red queens. That scoring combination was all he had worth anything among the five cards dealt him. He hissed inwardly in disgust. A pair was just above a random hand with nothing of scoring strength.

He gazed around at the other players, trying to gauge by their expressions and posture how good their hands were. Could they have gotten even worse hands? Was that possible?

The small man was tapping the table with his left hand and looking at Lon in an odd way. Lon decided he would lay two cards facedown and deal himself another two. He hoped they'd be better than the pitiful ones he'd dealt himself first.

The miner hit the other man's hand, which was tapping beside him. "Stop that. You tryin' to fiddle with my concentration?"

Lon held his breath. He'd seen fights start with less provocation than this.

The small man hit back the offending hand. "If you been drinking too much, don't take it out on me."

The miner lurched forward.

Fortunately, the onlookers voiced loud disapproval of the fight—it would spoil their fun. The miner scowled but sat back in his chair.

Reminding himself of the pistol in his vest pocket, Lon put two cards facedown and drew two more cards. His pair of queens became a triple, two red and one black. *Better. But not much.*

Then, as the dealer, he went from player to player asking if they wanted to draw again. There was another round of calling and betting. The small man was still watching Lon with an intense gaze. Was there going to be trouble?

The man asked, "You fight in the war?"

Lon shrugged. "Most of us did, didn't we?"

This appeared to aggravate the small man even more. He looked at Lon with narrowed eyes. Lon tried to ignore him. Winning the game was what mattered. Nothing was going to distract him from that.

The final round ended and each player laid down his cards. Lon wished he could have had another chance to make his hand better, but he laid down his three queens. And nearly broke his poker face when he saw that he had won. Victory and relief flowed through him.

The sullen miner's face twisted in anger. "You sure you're not dealing from the bottom of the deck?"

Lon looked at him coolly. "If you don't want me to deal, you deal." He began shuffling the cards with rapid and practiced hands. The men standing around liked to watch someone who could handle cards as well as he could. He didn't hold back, letting the cards cascade from one hand to the other and then deftly working the cards like an accordion. He held his audience in rapt attention.

The young Métis who'd lost his gambling money rose, and another man slid into his place. Lon nodded to him and began dealing cards for another game. One of the saloon girls came over and tried to drape herself around Lon's shoulders. Not wishing to be impolite, he murmured, "Not while I'm working, please, miss." She nodded and moved over to lean on the dark-haired miner.

Lon hoped she would sweeten the man's temper but the miner shrugged her off with a muttered insult. Lon looked at the cards he'd dealt himself and nearly revealed his shock. He held almost a royal flush: jack, queen, king, ace and a four.

The odds of his dealing this hand to himself were incredible. The other players turned cards facedown and he dealt them the number of cards they requested. Lon put the four down and drew another card. He stared at it, disbelieving.

The betting began. Lon resisted the temptation to bet the rest of his money on the game. That would signal to the other players that he had good cards, which in this case was a vast understatement. He bet half the money he had just won. The other players eyed him and each raised. The second round of betting took place. Then Lon concealed his excitement and laid out the royal flush—ten, jack, queen, king, ace.

He reached forward to scoop up the pot. The small man leaped from his seat, shouting, "You can't have dealt honestly. No one gets a royal flush like that!"

Lon eyed the man. He'd played cards several times with him over the past days, and the man had been consistently even-tempered.

"You're right!" The dark-haired miner reared up from his chair and slammed a fist into Lon's face. Lon flew back into the men crowding around the table. He tried to find his feet, but he went down hard on one knee. He leaped up again, his fists in front of his face.

The gold and silver coins he'd just won were clinking, sliding down the table as the miner tipped it over. "No!" Lon bellowed. "No!"

The miner swung again. Lon dodged, getting in two good jabs. The miner groaned and fell. Then the small mustached man pulled a knife from his boot.

A knife. Lon leaped out of reach again. He fumbled for the Derringer in his vest. The small man jumped over the upended table. He plunged his knife into Lon just above the high pocket of his vest.

As his own warm blood gushed under his hand, Lon felt himself losing consciousness. The crushing pain in his chest made it hard to breathe. He looked at the man nearest him, a stranger. He was alone in this town of strangers.

No, I'm not.

Lon blinked, trying to get rid of the fog that was obscuring his vision. "Get the woman doctor," he gasped. "Get Dr. Gabriel."

Chapter Four

Pounding. Pounding. Mercy woke in the darkness, groggy. More sights and sounds roused her—the sound of a match striking, a candle flame flickering to life, padding footsteps going toward the curtains. "Aunt Mercy, get up," Indigo commanded in the blackness. "Someone's nearly breaking down the front door and shouting for the doctor." The curtain swished as Indigo went through it to answer the door.

Mercy sat up. Feeling around in the darkness, she started getting dressed without thinking, merely reacting to Indigo's command. With her dress on over her nightgown, she sat down to pull on her shoes. She found she was unable to lift her stockinged feet. The listlessness which had gripped her over the past week smothered her in its grasp once more.

She had not left the mining office—in fact, could not leave it. She knew her lassitude had begun to worry Indigo. Her daughter had given her long looks of bewildered concern. Yet Mercy had been unable to reassure Indigo, had been unable to break free from the lethargy, the hopelessness, the defeat she'd experienced deep, deep inside. And somehow it had been connected with Lon Mackey, but why?

With the candle glowing in front of her face, Indigo came in with three men crowding behind her. "Aunt Mercy, Lon Mackey has been knifed in the saloon."

Cold shock dashed its way through Mercy. As if she'd been tossed into water, she gasped and sucked in air.

"It's serious. We must hurry." Indigo set the candlestick on the potbellied stove and began pulling a dress on over her nightgown. Then in the shadows, she bent, opened the trunk at the end of the room and pulled out two black leather bags, one with surgical items and one with nursing supplies.

Mercy sat, watching Indigo by the flickering candlelight. Her feet were still rooted to the cold floor.

"Ain't you gonna get up, lady—I mean, lady doctor?" one of the men asked. "The gambler's unconscious and losing blood. He needs a doc."

Indigo turned and snagged both their wool shawls from a nail on the wall. "Aunt Mercy?"

"Yeah," one of the other men said, "the gambler asked for you—by name. Come on."

He asked for me. The image of Lon bleeding snapped the tethers that bound her to the floor. Mercy stirred, forcing off the apathy. She slid her feet into her shoes and dragged herself up. "Let's go."

Outside for the first time in days, she shivered in the October night air, shivered at once more being outside, vulnerable. Thinking of Lon and recalling how he'd done whatever she needed, whatever she'd asked during the cholera outbreak, she hurried over the slick, muddy street toward the saloon. In the midst of the black night, oil lamps shone through the swinging door and the windows, beckoning.

The men who'd come to get them hurried forward, shouting out, "The lady doc is coming!"

Mercy and Indigo halted just outside the door. Having difficulty drawing breath, Mercy whispered, "Pray." Indigo nodded and they entered side by side. The bright lights made Mercy blink as her eyes adjusted. Finally, she discerned where the crowd was thickest.

She headed straight toward the center of the gathering, her steps jerky, as if she were walking on frozen feet. "Nurse Indigo," she said over her shoulder, "get the bar ready for me, please." But a glance told her that Indigo was already disinfecting the bar in preparation.

The gawking men parted as Mercy swept forward. One unfamiliar man popped up in front of her. "Hold it. A woman doctor? She might do him more harm than good."

Before Mercy could respond, the dissenting man

was yanked back and shoved out of her way, the men around all chorusing, "The gambler asked for her."

Unchecked, Mercy continued, her strength coming back in spurts like the blood surging, pulsing through her arteries. Her walking smoothed out.

She had never doctored with such a large crowd pressing in on every side. She sensed the men here viewed this as a drama, a spectacle. Still, she kept her chin up. If they'd come to see the show, she'd show them all right.

Then she saw Lon. He had been stretched out on a table, a crimson stain soaking the front of his white shirt and embroidered vest. An invisible hand squeezed the breath from her lungs and it rushed out in a long "Oh."

A young woman in a low-cut, shiny red dress was holding a folded towel over the wound. She looked into Mercy's eyes. "This was all we had to stop the bleeding."

Mercy nodded, drawing up her reserves. "Excellent." She put her black bag on the table beside Lon and lifted out the bottle of wood alcohol. She poured it over both her trembling hands, hoping to quiet her nerves as she disinfected. To hide the quivering of her hands, she shook them and then balled them into fists. "Let me see the wound, please."

The young woman lifted the blood-soaked towel and stepped back. She was the only one who did so— everyone else pressed in closer. "Please, friends," Mercy stated in a firm tone, forcing the quavering from her voice, "I must have room to move my arms. I must have light. Please."

The crowd edged back a couple of inches. The girl in the low-cut dress lifted a lamp closer to Lon.

Mercy wished her inner quaking would stop. She sucked in more air laden with cigar smoke, stale beer and sweat. She looked down into Lon's face.

She had tended so many bleeding men in the war, yet her work then had been anonymous. She had never before been called to tend someone whom she knew and whom she had depended on, worked with. Seeing a friend like this must be what was upsetting her. She must focus on the wound, not the man.

In spite of her trembling fingers, Mercy unbuttoned and tugged back his shirt. She examined the wound and was relieved to see that the blood was clotting and sluggish. The wound, though deep, had not penetrated the heart or abdomen. That would have been a death sentence. Her shaking lessened. This was her job, this was what she had been called to do.

As she probed the wound, she felt a small part of the lung that may have collapsed. She had read about pulmonary atelectasis—once she closed the wound, the lung would either reinflate or compensate. But she needed to act quickly.

She turned toward the bar. "Nurse Indigo, is my operating table ready?"

"Almost, Dr. Gabriel." While working in public, both women used these terms of address. The dean of the Female Medical College of Pennsylvania had insisted on using their titles to imbue them with respect.

"Please carry the patient to the bar, and bring my bag, too," Mercy asked of the men. "I will operate there." Mercy turned and the way parted before her. She was accustomed to disbelief and disapproval, but never before had she been forced to endure being put on display. Her face was hot and glowing bright scarlet.

She had heard of circuses that had freak shows, displaying bearded women and other humans with physical abnormalities. Here she was the local freak, the lady doctor. But her concern for Lon's survival outweighed her embarrassment and frustration. He was depending on her.

For a moment, she felt faint. She scolded herself for such weakness and plowed her way to the bar. Now Indigo was helping the bartender position the second of two large oil lamps.

"How bad is it, Doctor?" Indigo asked.

"Can you do anything for him? Or is he a goner?" asked the bartender.

The word *goner* tightened Mercy's throat. "The wound may have collapsed part of the lung. I will need to stitch up the wound."

There was a deep murmuring as everyone made their opinion of this known, discussing it back and forth. Mercy focused on Lon and her task. In the background, the voices blended together in a deep ebb and flow, like waves on a shore.

Indigo laid out the surgical instruments on a clean linen cloth. Mercy looked to the saloon girl, who was hovering nearby. "What is thy name, miss?"

"Sunny, ma'am—I mean, Doc."

"Sunny, will thee help me by unbuttoning the shirt and vest the rest of the way and helping the bartender remove them? I must scrub my hands thoroughly before I begin surgery."

Sunny nodded and began undoing Lon's vest buttons.

Mercy moved farther down the bar, where Indigo had poured boiled water and alcohol into a clean basin. She picked up a bar of soap and began scrubbing her hands and nails with a little brush, hating each moment of delay.

"Hey, Lady Doc," one of the men asked, his voice coming through the constant muttering, "shouldn't you wash up *after* you mess with all the blood and stuff?"

Mercy kept scrubbing as she addressed his question. "A young English doctor, Joseph Lister, has discovered that mortality rates decline in hospitals that practice antiseptic measures before surgical procedures."

"Really? Is that a fact?" the man said. "What's *antiseptic* mean?"

"*Sepsis* is when a wound becomes infected, and it usually leads to the patient's death. *Anti* means against, so antiseptic measures try to prevent sepsis."

"My ma always said cleanliness is next to godliness," another man spoke up.

"Thy mother was a wise woman. In my experience, women with cleaner houses lose fewer children to disease."

Mercy held out her hands, and Indigo poured more boiled water and then wood alcohol over them. Mercy took a deep breath and turned to her task. "Nurse Indigo, will thee please spray the patient with carbolic acid?"

Using the large atomizer, Indigo sprayed carbolic acid over Lon's broad chest and then directly over the wound, which she had already sponged clean of gore. Mercy proceeded to inspect Lon's wound, feeling for the deepest point. There was silence all around her—thick, intent silence—as everyone watched her every move. She located the point, reached for her needle and silk thread and began to close the wound with tiny stitches.

"Hey! Look!" a man called out. "She's doin' it. Look!"

Mercy felt the press of the crowd. "*Please,* thee must all move back. I must have room to work." *To breathe.*

The men edged back. She drew in air and prayed on silently. She could only hope that Indigo's pressure, plus natural clotting and healing, would help seal the wound and allow the lung to reinflate.

Mercy set and tied her final stitch and blinked away tears she couldn't explain. She was thankful that Lon hadn't stirred during the probing or suturing.

"You done, Lady Doc?" the bartender asked.

"Yes. Now we must hope that Lon Mackey will sleep a bit longer, then wake and begin to heal. Do any of thee know where Lon has been staying?"

"He's bunking in the back room," Sunny said.

Mercy had wondered where Lon roomed. And though his living arrangement fit his gambling, she could not like Lon in this place. She pursed her lips momentarily.

"I suggest that he be carried to his bed, then," Mercy said. "Nurse Indigo and I will take turns staying with him."

A censorious voice came from behind. "Decent women don't hang around bars."

Mercy turned and recognized the speaker as the same man who had tried to prevent her from treating Lon. "I am a doctor. I know my job, and I do it wherever my patient is."

She turned her back on the disapproving man, who had a distinctive shock of gray hair. She wouldn't forget him any time soon. "Please, some of thee carry Lon to his bed very carefully. I don't want sudden jarring to disturb the wound."

Several men lifted Lon from the bar. He moaned. The men halted. Though Lon's eyelids fluttered, he didn't revive. Mercy waved the men on and she followed them. It wasn't uncommon for a person to remain unconscious for a long while after surgery, but Mercy prayed that Lon wouldn't remain asleep for many more hours.

She had just displayed her abilities to many. The outcome of her surgery must be positive, or she might be forced to leave this place in disgrace.

This cold thought brought back the trembling deep inside. She had done for Lon what he needed her to do, and now she needed him to get well. *I need thee to wake up and move, Lon Mackey, our only friend here. Please wake up.*

Lon realized that he was breathing, just barely. Something wasn't right. He felt pain, like his chest was on fire. Like it had been crushed. He recalled loud voices and a table tipping. Something bad had happened. He tried to open his eyes but the lids were heavy, so heavy. Finally, he managed.

He blinked several times to rid himself of the fog that clung to his senses. Then he saw her. Just a few feet from him, Mercy sat in a chair, her eyes closed. He squinted. What was Mercy doing sitting beside his bed? In the back of the saloon? Was he hallucinating?

He tried to speak and couldn't. What had happened? He couldn't gather his thoughts. They were like popcorn sizzling in a hot pan, hopping and jumping out of reach. His face felt like it was that hot pan. A fever? Had the cholera got him this time?

He looked to Mercy. Maybe she would speak to

him and then he would know what had happened, why his chest hurt, why he couldn't speak. But Mercy's eyes remained closed. Her thick, golden-brown lashes fanned out against her pale skin. She'd taken off her bonnet. Her flaxen hair had slipped from the tight bun at the nape of her neck. Her small nose was pointed downward; her pale-pink lips were parted slightly. He couldn't look away. How lovely she was. How untouched.

He drew a deep breath. Pain stabbed his chest. He stopped the flow of air, then let it out slowly, slowly. He lifted his hand, or tried to. "Mercy," he whispered. "Mercy."

Her eyelids fluttered and opened. "Lon." She leaned forward in her chair. "Lon, how is thee feeling?"

He moistened his mouth and tried to speak again.

"Thy mouth is dry, Lon Mackey." She reached over, lifted a cast-iron kettle and filled a cup. "Here. Drink this. It has more to it than water and thee needs strength. If thee can stay awake, I have venison broth ordered for thee."

He drank the lukewarm, bitter coffee with gratitude. He hadn't realized how thirsty he was until he had seen her pouring coffee into the cup. "More."

She refilled the cup and he swallowed it down, lay back, gasping as if he'd just sprinted a mile.

"What happened?" he whispered.

"Thee suffered an injury. Does thee want some venison broth?"

"Yes." He wasn't hungry, but he knew eating was necessary.

Mercy rose. "Sunny!"

He heard footsteps and turned his head. The petite blonde came down the stairs. "Yes, Doctor?"

"Will thee go to the café and ask for broth for my patient? The proprietress said she would keep some on the stove for me."

"Of course, Doctor."

"I thank thee. I don't know why Indigo hasn't returned."

Lon remembered then. This blonde girl had been there when—what had happened? "What kind of injury?" Hearing his own words startled him.

"Thee was stabbed." Mercy's voice was matter-of-fact.

"Stabbed? By whom?"

"I do not know. I did not see it happen. I was called to the saloon to doctor thee."

He rolled her answers around in his mind like marbles, but he could call up no memory. Mercy wouldn't lie, so it must be true. Anger flickered in him. Had the man been apprehended? The fog was blowing into his mind again. *No, no, let me think…*

Lon woke to Mercy's coaxing voice. "Lon, Lon, thy broth has come. It's nice and hot, and smells delicious. Please open thy eyes."

He looked up into her face and was swamped with the comfort of seeing her. He stiffened himself against the pull toward her. *I'm weak and getting strange thoughts. It's just good to have a friend, and one who's a doctor.* He tried to raise himself. Pain lanced down his left side. He couldn't stop a groan. "Help me sit up."

"Friend," Mercy said in that tone people used with children and invalids, "thee were stabbed, remember? That will pain thee on the left side. Let me raise thy head and I will help thee with the broth."

"I'm a grown man. I don't need help eating," he snapped. The words exhausted him. If he'd had the strength, he would have cursed. *No, not in front of Mercy.*

"Thee is weak from thy wound. Thy blood loss was considerable. Thy strength will return if thee will only let me help." Mercy slid another pillow under his head and shoulders. Then she picked up the bowl and spooned some broth into his mouth.

The broth was salty and hot. It made him feel better as it coursed down his throat. He wanted to tell her again that he could feed himself. Then he realized he was wrong.

"How soon," he asked, swallowing between spoonfuls, "will I be up again?"

"I cannot say. All I know is that thee will need careful nursing. Thee will need to eat as often as thee can and drink plenty of liquids. Thee has a fever, which is completely normal under these circumstances."

He wanted to ask, *Can I still die?* But he didn't. Of course he could still die. They both knew that from the war. His fever was due to infection, and infection could kill him. He fought the rush of moisture to his eyes.

"After thee has drunk this broth, I will begin fomenting thy wound. It will help keep thy fever down—"

"How's Mackey doing?" the bartender interrupted as he entered from the rear of the saloon. He held out his hand. "I'm Tom, remember?"

Mercy began to reply, but Lon cut her off. He could speak for himself. "I'll be up in no time." His bravado cost him.

The hearty red-faced bartender had the nerve to chuckle. "Yeah, well, I hope so. I like having an honest gambler in the place. It's good for business."

"Did the man who stabbed me get arrested?" Lon asked, feeling his thin vitality leak out with each word.

"He took off and we couldn't find him," Tom said. "We telegraphed his description to the territorial sheriff in Boise. That's about all we can do."

Lon made a sound of disgust and then sipped another spoonful of broth, hating that he needed to be fed.

"Friend," Mercy said, looking at the bartender, "I am concerned about Lon Mackey staying here at night. He needs his sleep, and the noise from the saloon will keep him awake."

"I slept all night, didn't I?" Lon demanded, regretting it instantly. Every time he spoke, it sapped energy from him.

Tom folded his arms and leaned against the unpainted, raw wood wall. "I see what you mean, Doc. But there's not many places available."

Lon forced himself to stay silent and just swallow the broth. He couldn't afford to waste more effort on words. He stopped listening to the conversation. Feeling her soft palm on his forehead, he turned into it and let himself enjoy the sensation. The fever had wrapped him in its heat.

He had been wounded before and knew that the pain would pass—if his luck held. He'd made it through nearly four years of war. Thousands of others hadn't. He tried to block out the images of battle and the charge of fear that they brought. *The war's over. It's done. Maybe I'm done.* He didn't like that last idea. *She doesn't think I'm done.*

He managed to open his eyes enough to glance up into Mercy's face. Did she know how pretty she was? He noticed that she had a widow's peak that made her face heart-shaped. Her blue eyes looked down at him with deep concern. And compassion. How could she care so much about strangers? How had the two of them ended up in this place? Hadn't she seen enough of pain, misery and death in the war?

His leaden eyelids drifted down. Maybe the answer

lay in the fact that while she had nursed the wounded and dying, she hadn't ordered them into the line of fire and watched them die. Consciousness began to slip from him and he welcomed oblivion, even as he fought to stay awake, stay alive. There was something about this woman that made him want to live. Why hadn't her father kept her at home and married her off to some neighboring farmer, out of harm's way?

Out of my way?

After the bartender went to unshutter the front door for another day's business, Mercy looked at Lon as he slid into sleep. He'd almost finished the broth, and that was heartening. Even his crankiness was a good sign. She stood and stretched her back and neck.

"Hello!" a woman's voice came from outside the front door. "Is the lady doctor here?"

Mercy sent one last glance at Lon and then walked through the saloon. Outside, she saw a large, blowsy woman, one of those who had refused to let her board. Mercy approached her with caution.

"Good day, may I help thee?"

Something beyond the woman caught Mercy's eye: Indigo, across the street, down a few storefronts. She was talking to a man.

"Remember me? I'm Ma Bailey. You still looking for a place to board?" the big woman asked.

Mercy was incredulous. *She wouldn't take us in a*

week ago. Now she wants us. Why? "We have been staying in the back of the mining—"

"Know that. But you can't stay there forever. It's not a house. I got room for you in my place. Two dollars a week. That includes food. You got to go to the Chinese for laundry. What do you say?"

"I will consider your offer." *Your belated offer.* The woman looked disgruntled, glancing up and down as if she had more to say.

Gazing at Indigo over the woman's shoulder, Mercy waited for her to come to the point. Indigo was behaving in a most unusual fashion while speaking to the man. It suddenly struck Mercy that Indigo was flirting. Mercy wished the young man would turn around so she could see his face. Indigo and she had never discussed it, but as a woman of color, Indigo faced special risks with white men. But she couldn't see the color of his skin. There were men called half breeds in town. She had yet to see a black man hereabouts.

"Ya see, it's this way," Ma interrupted. "My daughter and her man are coming here before winter. Just got a letter when the supply wagons came in today. And she's expecting." Ma Bailey looked up at her, suddenly beaming. "I was thinking that when her time comes, she could use a good midwife. The first baby's always the hardest. I mean, you don't know if she'll have an easy time or not."

Ah, now this makes sense. Self-interest is *always*

a good bet when guessing a person's motivation. "Whether I board in thy home or not, I will be happy to attend to thy daughter's first delivery."

"Yeah, but it's like this." Ma hemmed and hawed with the best of them. "I was thinkin' you might give us a deal on the cost, since you'd be livin' with me."

Mercy gave the woman a thin smile. Stinginess, another reliable incentive for some. Did she want to live with a grasping, unkind, prejudiced woman? No, she did not. "My fees are not exorbitant. I'm sure thy son-in-law will be able to meet them. I thank thee for thy invitation."

The man Indigo was flirting with turned a bit, but his hat cast a shadow over his face. *Be careful, Indigo.*

In spite of Mercy's obvious wish to conclude the conversation, the woman lingered. "You really patched up that gambler?"

"I did indeed," Mercy said.

"Never heard the like. You must really know what you're doing."

"I studied for three years at the Female Medical College of Pennsylvania and passed all the tests."

The woman shook her head. "That beats all. Women doctors. What will they think of next?" She walked away, calling over her shoulder, "Let me know when you make up your mind."

But Mercy was studying the young man's tall, lean profile. And then Indigo glanced toward her and quickly looked away. Mercy hoped the gentleman would turn out to be a fine young man with courting on his mind. She should have been expecting something like this—Indigo would be sixteen on Christmas Day, just the right age to start thinking of romance.

Yet Indigo was at risk. Mercy hadn't yet seen any men of color in the Idaho Territory, and some white men would be more than willing to take advantage of Indigo's innocence. Even if they were serious about her, mixed marriages were unheard-of and could unleash the nastiest kind of race hate. Mercy had realized that her life's mission didn't include a husband. A doctor was at the beck and call of everyone. How could a woman care for a house, children and a husband with such a demanding schedule? So Mercy hadn't given Indigo's future much thought. However, she didn't want to force her spinsterhood onto her daughter. Her observations today gave her a new concern to consider and to address.

Her thoughts turned to Lon, and she headed back to check on him. She walked into the back room and found Sunny sitting in her chair. Some strong emotion rocked Mercy. She paused for a moment, letting the unusual feeling lap over her like sea waves. She realized that she didn't like finding Sunny alone with Lon.

And then she noticed that Sunny was evidently trying to hide the fact that she was expecting. She looked to be near her last trimester. When the girl was standing, it wasn't so evident. But sitting, yes, it was unmistakable.

Sunny glanced up and then popped out of Mercy's chair. "I was just watching him while you were gone, Doc."

Mercy nodded. She forced herself from the clutches of her unusual reaction, and then pity came swiftly. This young woman, who was just a few years older than Indigo, was going to need help soon. The world was not kind to babies born out of wedlock. More than once, Mercy's parents had welcomed young girls in this situation into their home. Mercy thought of her sister, Felicity, who was running an orphanage.

Mercy smiled kindly at Sunny. "I thank thee. My nurse will come soon to relieve me."

Mercy watched the young woman leave, wondering how to speak with her about her condition, a condition that she hoped Indigo would never find herself in without a good husband to look after her.

Lon Mackey stirred, and Mercy waited to see if he were about to wake. She felt a rush of tenderness toward the man who had stood by her when she'd first come to town. Despite his unusual choice of profession, the man had the potential to make a woman a very good husband, since he seemed to take a woman at her word and didn't mind if she knew more than he.

Lon's eyes opened and he caught her gazing

at him. She didn't have time to look away, so she smiled instead. After a moment, he smiled back at her. Warmth flooded her face as he slowly slid back into sleep.

Chapter Five

Late that night, Mercy woke once again to the sound of pounding on her door. Would that sound ever stop making her heart race? She lit the bedside candle and padded on bare feet to open the door. "Yes?" she asked, shivering in the cool draft that made the candle flicker.

"Please, you come. Please. Wife bad. Baby not come."

This speech was delivered by a young Chinese man. Still waking up, Mercy stared at the man. Was this a dream?

"Please, you come. I pay. Wife bad. Baby not come. People say you doctor, good doctor."

Mercy snapped awake. "One moment." Leaving the door open, she pulled her sadly wrinkled dress on over her nightgown, then slid into her shoes and grabbed her bag. She wished Indigo were here, but she was watching over Lon Mackey, who **was still** feverish and sometimes delirious in the rear of the saloon.

Mercy stepped outside. Shivering again in the moonlight, she locked the door behind her. "Please lead the way. I'll do what I can for thy wife and baby."

The man bowed twice and then took off running down the dark alley. Mercy hurried to keep up with him. After a week of idleness, even a late-night call was welcome. If she weren't so tired, she would have rejoiced.

Then the stress of this call punched her with its ugly fist. Childbirth loomed over all physicians as the leading cause of death among young females. She began praying as she hurried through the chill darkness, *Father, be with me tonight. Give me wisdom and skill.*

She was aware that there were Chinese immigrants in town. Ma Bailey had mentioned earlier that Mercy would have to take her laundry to the Chinese. How had these people found their way to the Idaho Territory? And why?

Before long, the two of them arrived at the far end of town, where a group of small wooden houses had been built very close together. The Chinese quarter was, of course, set apart from the rest of the town.

The man opened the door of one of these houses; a lamp was burning low inside. Two Chinese women were in the room, one sitting beside another who was lying in bed, obviously pregnant and in distress.

Mercy's nerves tightened another notch. Had she been called in too late? Would she be able to save both mother and child?

There was a flurry of rapid Chinese. Mercy pulled off her wool shawl and tossed it onto a peg on the wall. Then she turned to the man. "Water. I need hot water. *Now.*"

He hesitated only a moment to repeat her request. When she nodded her approval, he hurried outside. She turned to her patient whose face was pale and drawn, and whose hair was damp with perspiration, all signs of a prolonged labor. "I am Dr. Mercy Gabriel." Then she gestured to each of the women and asked, "And thee are?"

The man returned with a bucket of water and hung it over the fire in the hearth as he answered for the women. "I am Chen Park. She Chen An, wife. The other, friend, Lin Li." He bowed again.

Mercy repeated the names and nodded. She began to lay out her birthing instruments on the table with a trembling hand.

The young wife shouted again as an evidently strong labor pain gripped her.

"How long has she been in labor?" Mercy asked.

"Before dawn. I worry."

Nearly twenty-four hours of labor. Her hope for a healthy birth dimmed, but there was still hope for a live birth. Praying, Mercy nodded and washed her hands in the basin he'd just filled with fresh water. *Please, Father, let the child and mother live.*

She motioned for the lamp to be held near and examined her patient. Chen An moaned and whimpered. Mercy didn't blame her. She used her stethoscope to listen for the baby's heartbeat. She thought she heard it, but the mother's crescendo of moaning made it difficult.

"The baby is lodged in the birth canal." Buzzing inside with worry, Mercy went to her instruments and selected a long, narrow forceps.

They looked at her questioningly.

"The baby is stuck, can't get out. I will help baby come out." Mercy demonstrated how she would use the forceps. She didn't like using pidgin English and sign language, but she didn't have time for a long explanation.

Praying still, she sprayed carbolic acid around the birthing site, made a quick, small incision, and proceeded to use the forceps. The woman writhed and moaned, obviously calling for help. When Mercy sensed the next contraction, she gently applied pressure and righted the baby's head in the birth canal.

Chen An called out louder, frantic. Mercy held the child in place. "One more, Chen An," she coaxed. "One more push and this will be over."

The next contraction hit. Mercy held the forceps in place, keeping the baby from turning the wrong way. The baby slid onto the bed. A boy!

She dropped the forceps and cut the cord. Within

seconds, she had the baby wrapped in a white linen towel, suctioning out its mouth and nose. In the lamplight, the little face was so pale. Mercy slapped the bottom of the baby's feet. "Come on. Thee must breathe, little one." She slapped the small soles again. *Please. Please.*

Then in the silent, tense room, the baby gasped, choked and wailed. Chen Park whooped and laughed.

Mercy felt gratitude wash over her in great swells of relief. *Alive.* She couldn't help herself. She whirled on the spot like a girl, silently praising God for this new life.

She nestled the baby into the mother's arms. "Thee has a fine son, Mr. Chen Park," she said. "What will thee name him?"

"He will be called Chen Lee," the father pronounced, grinning.

Mercy nodded. "Hello, little Chen Lee. Welcome to this world, precious child."

Lon opened his eyes. Mercy was sitting in the chair beside his cot, smiling. The early morning light made her pale hair gleam with subtle gold. He admired the wide blue eyes that were looking at him with tenderness. The sight took his breath for a moment.

He'd spent the war and the past three years in saloons, far from respectable ladies like Mercy Gabriel. Nonetheless, his whole self experienced the pull toward her, toward the glimmering light, toward home and hearth…and peace.

He closed his eyes. *Get hold of yourself, man.*

"Good morning, friend." Her voice was low and velvety, kind to his ear. "Here's some tea for thee."

Her hands slid under his shoulders and added two more pillows. He turned his face to let her palm cup his cheek. *So stupid of me.* He broke the contact.

"Does thee think thee can hold thy cup today?"

He opened his eyes. "Yes." He accepted the cup, trying to keep it from shaking. The fever still burned inside him and the cup trembled in his hand.

She closed her soft hand over his, steadying it.

He braced himself to resist the feeling of her touch, of connectedness with this good woman. But the fever worked against him. If he tried to hold the cup himself, it would fall and break. Better to just let her hold it. "You can do it," he said ungraciously. He let his arm fall back to his side, free from her touch.

She held the cup to his lips. He sipped and then said, feeling disgruntled, "You look happy."

"I am. I had the privilege of helping a beautiful little baby boy safely into this world. He is little Chen Lee."

From what he had seen of the way the Chinese were treated here in the West, where they had immigrated to build the railroads, he thought that someday this little boy would rue the day he was born in the Idaho Territory. If he survived.

"I'm always happy when I deliver a baby alive and well. It's such a marvel." Mercy's face glowed.

He wanted to say something to bring her back to reality. He quoted harshly, "'For all flesh is as grass, and all the glory of man as the flower of grass. The grass withereth, and the flower thereof falleth away.'"

"Yes," she replied, "Peter wrote that. But Isaiah declared, 'The grass withereth, the flower fadeth: but the word of our God shall stand forever.'"

He cursed himself for bringing up a Bible verse. The idea of God was hard to let go of completely. But after four devastating, bloody years of war, if God was still there, Lon didn't like him very much.

"Where's Indigo?" he grumbled. *Let the subject of man and God drop, Mercy.*

Mercy nodded her head as if acceding to his unspoken request. "She has gone to take a nap. I will watch over thee this morning."

"Don't need someone watching over me."

The Quaker had the nerve to chuckle at him. "Thee will be better sooner if I am here to give thee tea, broth and maybe even oatmeal."

"Sounds delicious," he snapped and then took another sip of hot, sweet tea. It was appetizing and strengthening. He ground his teeth in seething frustration as hot as the fever he couldn't shake.

She chuckled again. "I know thee is the kind of man who doesn't want anyone fussing over him. I will not fuss, but someone must see that thee has liquid and nourishment often. Who else is there to do this, friend?"

He had no answer for her. He had made certain that he developed no friendships here. Now he wished he had befriended someone, anyone. Having this gentle, gracious woman nearby awoke so many memories from the past—his mother, sister and Janette... No, not Janette. His mind wouldn't let his memories of her intrude. He crushed them now without mercy. Janette had nothing in common with this caring doctor, save their gender.

Without Mercy. He must find a way to get better quickly and go back to gambling without this woman who made him long for the life he'd once known.

He tried not to think that this fever might best him yet. Had he survived four years of carnage only to be felled by a knife in a barroom brawl?

Later, Mercy glanced once more over her shoulder as she stepped from the back room of the saloon into the alley. Indigo was sitting beside Lon Mackey, who was sleeping again. Still a little drowsy herself from the interrupted night's sleep, Mercy walked around the front of the saloon and stood looking up and down the street, trying to decide how to find living quarters and an office. Then a thought occurred to her. Maybe what she was looking for wasn't on Main Street. She began to walk the long alleys on both sides of Main Street.

Her thoughts strayed back to Lon Mackey. Was his

crankiness just because he felt weak? Men didn't like to feel weak, especially not men like Lon. Or was he angry with her for some reason? The name Janette came to mind. Lon had uttered this name more than once in his delirious moments.

She shied away from thoughts of Lon Mackey's personal life—and the feelings those thoughts raised—and recalled last night's delivery. She looked toward the Chinese quarter. Out in the fresh air, men were working—boiling clothing in large washtubs over fires, hanging sheets on clotheslines. Some were ironing. She had never seen a man do laundry. She had never seen loose cotton clothes like the ones they were wearing. The sight fascinated her. Why had they come to live here in this place so far from home?

Of course, that was what she had done, too. Was a female doctor any more welcome here than a person of Chinese descent? She couldn't even rent a place to live.

The early autumn twilight was coloring the sky as she turned back and walked to the general store, where she had met Jacob Tarver. "Jacob Tarver," she greeted him, "I see that thee has a storeroom behind thy store."

He looked startled, then said, "Ah, yes."

"Have thee thought of renting it out?" she asked with a bright smile.

"I don't understand." He eyed her as if she'd just dropped from the sky.

Mercy explained to him that she wanted to rent

the storeroom for her medical practice. She talked on, overcoming his objection that he needed the storage space with the suggestion that he build a larger warehouse at the edge of town to stock his supplies, thereby increasing his income even more. He could rent her the rear storeroom for her medical practice and then rent out part of his new warehouse to other merchants.

And before she was done, she left him with the comfortable belief that this was what he had been intending to do all along. He promised to have the storeroom cleaned out and ready for her in a day or two.

Mercy would have felt guilty about this friendly persuasion except that it benefited Jacob Tarver as well. As she left the store, she heard a woman call her name. She recognized the pretty dark-haired mother of Missy.

"Miss Gabriel, I mean Dr. Gabriel," the young woman stammered, "I'm Mrs. James Dunfield, Ellen Dunfield. I have been so busy helping my husband and daughter regain their strength after the cholera and taking care of my infant son that I didn't realize that you had been sleeping in the mining office. Please, you must come and stay in our vacant cabin. My husband did so well in panning for gold that he built us a regular house. But the cabin is in good repair and will be a snug home for you this winter."

Joy lifted Mercy. "God bless thee, Ellen Dunfield. Yes, Indigo and I are still looking for a place to stay."

"Well, my Jim and I talked it over, and we don't care what anybody says about mixing races. You and that Indigo saved our family, and we don't give bad for good. And having an able midwife in town is good news for all us wives."

Concentrating on the positive sentiment behind Ellen Dunfield's words, Mercy asked for directions to the cabin and told Ellen that Indigo would bring their things soon and thanked the woman again. Mercy walked back toward the saloon. *Why did I give in to despair? God is in this place, too.*

Three nights later, Mercy supervised while Lon was moved to the new office, where a bed had been set up for him. The storeroom was large enough for an office, a treating room with an examining table and a bed for patients who needed nursing but had no family to provide it.

A stout black stove had been added to the storeroom. Everything was new, clean and neat. Though pleased with her first formal office, Mercy had no time to admire her surroundings. She turned her thoughts to Lon. His fever wouldn't let go. If she couldn't break his fever…

Lon mumbled. He was somewhere between waking and sleeping. Mercy wished this move had not been necessary on such a chilly night, when he was still so vulnerable. But autumn was progressing and there was no holding it back. And this quiet place would be better for him. The loud nights in the back room of the saloon had been a trial.

"Thank thee, friends. Thank thee much," Mercy said to the volunteers.

"Our pleasure, Doc," one of the older men said. Then he hurried out the door as if this kind act were a form of mischief he might be caught doing.

She shook her head and then shivered sharply. November had come today, and the crisp air was penetrating. She added another log to the stove and then sat down in a rocking chair she'd purchased the day before. She wet a cloth with wood alcohol and bathed Lon's face with it. The heat from his skin warmed her hand.

This fever could kill him. The thought opened a deep abyss within her. She prayed aloud, "Father, I know this fever always comes with surgery. How can I break this good man's fever?"

She bathed his neck and wrists with the alcohol. *Lon, keep fighting. Don't give in.*

"Janette," Lon mumbled, "Janette."

That woman's name again. Mercy froze in place, hand on his arm. He mumbled the name a few more times and then spoke with agitation. Mercy only heard, "Wait…heart…Thomas…fickle."

Inside her came an explosion of feelings. Her heart pounded. Her breath became shallow and short. A startling realization she couldn't ignore pierced her.

I care for this man, this gambler. No, she couldn't let this be true. *No.*

"Mercy," Lon interrupted her. His eyes had opened.

His voice shocked her as much as the unexpected feelings that had welled up because he had said the name of another woman. Clamping down on the riot inside her, she braced herself and assured him, "I am here, Lon Mackey. Thee is in my new office."

"Thirsty."

She lifted his head and helped him drink a full glass of water. Tendrils of unwanted feelings made the act torturous. "Can thee drink more?"

"Tea?"

She busied herself at the stove where a cast-iron kettle sat. She made a pot of sweet tea and sat down. Lon drank the cup of tea eagerly. She stopped her unruly fingers from smoothing back his tousled hair.

"You shouldn't have to take care of me like this," he said in a harsh tone. His eyelids slid down. She touched his hot forehead with her wrist. He was awake enough to turn his head from her touch. She tried not to take offense at his rudeness. But it was hard not to, especially now when she sensed that she felt more than friendship for him.

What had caused this overwhelming cloudburst of feeling? Could she be feeling jealousy?

Mercy's innate honesty forced her to look at her

reaction without equivocation. Did she have a right to feel jealous over Lon? Of course not.

But she did. Mercy sat back in her rocker and closed her eyes. Where had this come from? Why hadn't she realized the direction her emotions were taking? And how could she stop this imprudence before it went any further?

Over two weeks later, as the local café was just brewing its first morning coffee, Lon knocked on the door of Mercy's office. *Dr. Gabriel's office.* Not *Mercy's.* Thinking of her as "the Quaker" might be a better, more aloof way to think of her. He stepped inside.

The Quaker looked up from her desk and smiled. Recovered from his fever, he had taken pains to present himself freshly shaved and sheared, dressed in his brushed and ironed gambler's clothing.

He would pay his bill for this doctor's service and make sure that she didn't think of him as anything except an acquaintance, a former patient. And then he'd go back to his life in the saloon. "You look as if you've been up all night," he said gruffly. He immediately regretted it, since it revealed his concern for her.

"The Dunfield baby had a fever last night. His parents have been so good to let us rent their cabin, I could not but help them. I just stopped here to leave a note that anyone needing the doctor should come to our cabin. Thee is looking well," she added, her blue eyes glowing with warmth.

He turned on the spot, as if showing off the suit to a prospective customer. "So glad you noticed, Miss Gabriel." Why had he called her that, as if she were some young lady he was interested in? "I mean, *Dr. Gabriel.*"

She tilted her head to one side, studying him.

Before she could speak, he said, "I've come to pay my bill." Some of the men who'd witnessed his stabbing had picked up his winnings and held them for him. It was nice to know a few decent men still walked the earth. A few.

She turned back to her desk and lifted out a paper, which she handed to him. He was slightly surprised that she had the bill ready. This must have shown on his face.

"I must earn a living, too, Lon Mackey. And I don't think I would make a very good gambler."

He wished she wouldn't look him in the eye, as she always did. It was unnerving. Young women just didn't look into a man's eyes. They had special ways of… How did a woman like this grow up without the slightest idea of how to entice a man? *Why am I thinking that?*

He pulled out his wallet and counted out her fee. She took the money from him, wrote "Paid in Full" and the date on the bill, and returned it to him, saying nothing. She just looked into his eyes.

Her blue eyes were her most attractive feature.

He gazed into them as if discerning afresh the innocence of her soul. Janette had blue eyes, too. This snapped him back to the present. "I'll bid you—"

"Are thee certain thee wants to return to the saloon?" she asked.

Her question ignited his irritation. Of course Dr. Mercy Gabriel would want to "save" him. "I like gambling," he retorted. "It's an easy life. No work. Nobody counting on me. I do what I like."

"An easy life as long as no one shoves a knife into thee again." Her tone was desert-dry.

"I don't expect you to understand me—"

"But I do understand thee," she interrupted him. "Were thee a major or a colonel?"

"A colonel." He gripped his walking stick, angry at his slip. "What has that got to do with anything?"

"I was in the war, too, thee recalls." She gazed up at him. "It isn't hard for me to see that thee... thee possesses the ability and habit of command. Thee took charge in the epidemic here and helped bring it to an end. I'm a doctor. I hold the lives of my patients in my hands. I understand the wish not to be responsible—"

Lon burned, and disliked the reaction. How could this woman understand him better than he did himself? He didn't want anybody's sympathy, much less that of this woman who wouldn't leave him alone—even when she wasn't in front of him.

Why couldn't he banish his concern for her? His awareness of her?

"You understand nothing." He turned and left.

Mercy rose and walked to the door Lon Mackey had slammed behind him. She walked out into the alley and glimpsed his back as he turned toward Main Street. The conversation had been brief in the extreme, but much had been revealed. The war had left its mark on their generation. Not just in the countless lives lost, but in all the shattered bodies, shattered dreams and shattered lives. And would the nightmares ever completely stop? Sometimes she still woke with her heart pounding, her ears ringing with cannon fire and a barrage of rifle fire. The sound of drums and the Rebel yell echoed in her mind. *Yet I didn't have to face battle and dread death, as Lon had. All I had to do was stand helplessly by and watch men die…* Mercy swallowed a moan of remembrance. No wonder Lon shied away from any connection to her or anyone else. No wonder.

Lon Mackey deserved a home, a loving wife and healthy children. When would the long, bitter fingers of the war release them all?

Down the alley, she glimpsed Indigo talking to that same man she had previously seen her with. Mercy stepped back into the doorway but was still able to observe them. She heard Indigo laugh. Evidently, love was in the fall air here in the Idaho Territory. Soon, Mercy would have to steel herself to speak to Indigo, to find out about this man who was making Indigo smile even when he wasn't near.

Suddenly, Jacob Tarver came around the corner of the building. "Miss Gabriel, I'm sorry! I hate that this has happened!"

"What has happened?" she gasped.

"Come on! It's all over the front window. I've never seen anything like it."

Picking up her skirts to run, Mercy followed the agitated man around to his storefront. All over his large front windows someone had used soap to print the words *Kick out the female doctor. Or else.* Scrawled under this was a string of curses.

Mercy stared at the words, stunned.

"I never thought anything like this would happen here," Jacob Tarver said.

Anger flashed through Mercy. "Coward!" she shouted.

Jacob Tarver jumped and stared at her.

"Not thee, Jacob Tarver. I'm not holding thee responsible," Mercy declared. She gestured angrily at the soap message. "Only a coward tries to frighten women!"

She swung around to glare at the crowd of people gathering in the street to gawk at the hot news of the day. "Does any of thee know who wrote this vile message? Does thee?"

Her mind sifted through all the people she'd met who had objected to her profession. She couldn't pinpoint one who stood out from the rest. Would this event lead to worse? Perhaps violence against her or against Indigo?

No one replied. Most looked worried. But a few looked pleased. Was it one of them? How could she find the culprit?

Chapter Six

Yesterday's ugly words had been scrubbed from the general store's front window, but not from Mercy's tender mind and heart. The same melancholy that had plagued her after the cholera epidemic was creeping over her, trying to imprison her again.

Mercy sat at the table in the snug log cabin. By the window's faint, gloomy light, Indigo was washing the breakfast dishes. Lon had recovered, which was good. But the shadow remained over her heart. *What am I to do? Why do I keep hearing Lon say, "You understand nothing"?*

"I know you're disheartened, Aunt Mercy," Indigo said, drying her hands on a dish towel and glancing over at Mercy.

Mercy smiled even as tears stung her eyes.

Indigo had taken a job as a waitress in one of the cafés in town to make extra money. Now she was leaving for work. Soon, Mercy was all alone in the cabin. Lifelong habit made her pick up her Bible. She turned to the Beatitudes, which her father had taught her was the best place to start when faced with a challenge. In the dim, lonely cabin, she read aloud, hearing her father's calm, measured voice in her mind.

Blessed are they which are persecuted for righteousness's sake: for theirs is the kingdom of heaven.

Blessed are ye, when men shall revile you, and persecute you, and shall say all manner of evil against you falsely, for my sake.

Rejoice, and be exceeding glad: for great is your reward in heaven: for so persecuted they the prophets which were before you...

Let your light so shine before men, that they may see your good works, and glorify your Father which is in heaven.

Mercy stroked the well-worn, black leather binding of the Bible. Words could be deeply loving, as her father's had always been to her and her sisters. Or they could be cruel because of the hate and fear behind them.

She thought she had become inured to the general objections to her joining what was deemed a "male" profession. Sometimes she even tried to be amused by the repeated litany of protests. But yesterday's offensive act took opposition against her to a new level of hostility.

Would the words on Jacob Tarver's window

keep sick people away from her when they needed doctoring?

"No," she said aloud. Yet she still did not want to go to her office. In fact, she felt as if bands were holding her back. She rose and carried the open Bible to the window. "I follow this unusual path because I was chosen to do this work. When the circumstances get desperate enough, they will come for my help."

This reminder triggered a new flow of confidence. She continued, "They needed me when the cholera was killing people. Lon Mackey needed me when he was stabbed. Chen An needed me to deliver her baby. How do I get them to come to me *before* the need is dire, Father?"

She looked down and her gaze fell on the verse, "Let your light so shine before men, that they may see your good works, and glorify your Father which is in heaven."

She glanced around her. Except for the faint light from the cabin's two windows and the glow of the low fire on the hearth, there was no light here.

Lon Mackey came to mind. But he always came to mind whenever she felt under stress. Could he help her here? Persuade others that since he'd fully recovered that she was a good doctor? That was tempting, but she didn't want to have to beg for help or involve Lon. He'd been through enough battles. She needed to face this one alone—or at least, without human help. God had never forsaken her. And hadn't now, either.

Closing her eyes, she prayed, *Father, let my light shine before men and let them praise Thee.* And to herself, she said, *I can stay here and wait for a special miracle, or I can proceed with one of my plans for this town right now, today. Release me from this holding back.* She resolutely closed her Bible, set it on the table and donned her shawl and bonnet.

If the people of Idaho Bend were not going to come to her, she would go to them. She stepped out into the dreary morning, trying to draw in the cool air. Her anxiety made it difficult to take more than shallow breaths.

With a decisive snap, Mercy shut the door of the cabin behind her. She approached the modest white-frame Dunfield house and tapped on the door. Young, pretty Ellen Dunfield, with her rich brown hair and matching eyes, answered the door. She was holding her one-year-old son with his halo of curly brown hair. Blonde, four-year-old Missy huddled close to her mother's side. "Dr. Gabriel, what can I do for you today?"

Courage. Mercy suppressed her uncertainty. "I just wanted to ask thee a question. Would thee be interested in learning more about the new ways of keeping thy family in good health?"

The young woman blinked. "What do you mean?"

"Great strides are being made in understanding how the body works and how to keep it healthy." Mercy infused her words with as much confidence as she could muster. Low, gray clouds hung overhead. Her breathing remained shallow. "Would thee, as the mother in thy home, be interested in learning some of these discoveries?"

"I'm terrible busy, ma'am."

Smiling, Mercy held up a hand. "I should have been more specific. What I would like to do is set up an afternoon meeting for townswomen, perhaps in one of the churches. I would have Indigo and a few other young girls babysit the children. Do thee think that thee would attend a meeting like this? Perhaps with tea served?"

Mrs. Dunfield pursed her lips, considering this. "There are new ways to keep children well?"

Gratefully, Mercy felt her lungs loosen. She was able to draw a deep breath. "Yes, there are. In Europe and America, doctors are learning more about the causes of disease and how to prevent it."

The boy interrupted by holding his arms out to Mercy. She reached out and took the child, who patted her cheek with a pudgy hand.

Missy looked up at Mercy. "You like babies, don't you, Dr. Mercy?"

Mercy chuckled. "Yes, I do."

"Why don't you got any?" Missy asked.

Mrs. Dunfield scolded Missy, "Hush! Where are your manners?"

"I don't have a husband," Mercy replied. "To have babies, there must be a father and a mother." She tapped Missy's nose, teasing.

"You are a good woman," Mrs. Dunfield announced, as if someone were there, disparaging Mercy. "I hate what that sneaky coward wrote on Mr. Tarver's window." The young woman glared at the unknown scoundrel. "So if you know ways for me to keep my family healthy, then I should learn them. What church will you be holding the meetings at?"

Mercy pushed on, her usual sturdy confidence nearly restored. "I was wondering if thee would ask thy pastor if I might use thy church building some afternoon next week, perhaps Friday at 2:00 p.m. I need time to let everyone know about the meeting."

"I will ask him," Mrs. Dunfield said. "I'm going to a prayer meeting tonight. I'll do it then."

"Excellent. And if he says I may, I will put an ad in the paper." The little boy babbled and Mercy handed him back. "Now I'm going to talk to a few of the other good mothers here in Idaho Bend and see if they would come."

"Can I go, too?" Missy asked.

Mrs. Dunfield hushed the child again.

"If thy mother doesn't need thee, I would be happy to have thee with me for company." Mercy looked to the mother.

"If she wouldn't be any trouble to you," Mrs. Dunfield said.

"Missy is no trouble at all," Mercy said. "Go get thy shawl, child. And we will set out to make our round of visits. I will have her home by lunchtime," Mercy assured the mother.

Soon she and Missy were walking down the rutted streets of the town, knocking on doors. Predictably, most of the women were hesitant or guarded, a few were hostile and a sparse few were enthusiastic. As they walked down Main Street, Ma Bailey flagged them down. "Why do you have the Dunfield girl with you?"

Mercy stared into the woman's pudgy face. Nosy, nosy, nosy. "Missy is accompanying me. Missy, why doesn't thee tell Mrs. Bailey why we are walking through town?"

"Dr. Mercy is going to teach lessons on how mamas can keep their children from getting sick. Will you come?"

"All children get sick," snapped Ma Bailey, ever the cheery ray of sunshine. "Have you found out who wrote those nasty words about you?" The woman didn't look upset, just eager for information.

Mercy tried to divine whether Ma Bailey knew the answer to her own question. "When does thee expect thy daughter and her husband to arrive?" she asked.

Worry etched itself into the deep lines of Ma Bailey's face. "I don't know, exactly. I'm so hopin' that they'll get here before she delivers. I heard you're good at deliverin' babies. I hear you even delivered a Chinese one." Ma Bailey frowned and shook her head, resuming her normal attitude of general disapproval.

"I'd never had the privilege of delivering a Chinese

baby before. And the baby's mother and father were
as thrilled with the birth of their son as thy daughter
and son-in-law will be with their newborn." Mercy
turned to leave this grumpy woman.

"What do you think of that half breed courtin'
your girl?" Ma Bailey's voice was sly.

Unable to speak, Mercy made no reply but merely
waved her hand and walked away with Missy. She
had not gotten a clear look at Indigo's beau, but had
thought he looked dark enough to have Indian blood.
She hated the demeaning phrase *half breed*.

When they had crossed the street, Missy said, "I
don't like that woman. She has mean eyes."

Mercy made no direct reply, but said, "I think we
will stop at Jacob Tarver's store and buy a certain
little girl a peppermint drop. What does thee think
of that idea?"

Missy smiled. "I like peppermint."

"I do, too. And I think thy mother might enjoy a
peppermint drop also." But Mercy's mind was preoc-
cupied with Ma Bailey's gnarly question. If Indigo's
interest in the young man, who evidently was of
mixed birth, was common gossip, then it was time
that she and Indigo discussed her future. There was
no getting around it any longer.

Lon walked out the saloon door and nearly collid-
ed with the Quaker and that little girl who'd survived
cholera. He cursed himself for not looking before
stepping outside the barroom's swinging door.

"Good day, Lon Mackey," the woman doctor greeted him.

"Hello, mister," the little girl said, waving up at him.

"Good day to you both." Though he wanted to, he couldn't bring himself to walk away. He fell into step with them, cursing his own weakness.

"We're going to the store for candy," the little girl said, skipping. "For peppermint candy."

"Aren't you a lucky little girl?" He felt like an idiot, saying those words.

"Where are you going?" the child asked.

"Missy, it is not polite to question grown-ups," Mercy said gently.

"I'm going to see if the supply wagons brought any recent newspapers," Lon replied.

The three of them arrived at the store. Mercy let Missy go inside to have time to enjoy gazing at the array of penny candy in the glass case. She looked up at Lon. "Have I offended thee, Lon Mackey?"

Her frank question bowled him over. He looked into her blue eyes and wished he hadn't. Her eyes were the windows to her soul, her pure, generous, selfless soul. "I am at fault," he admitted against his will. "I was abrupt to the point of rudeness. And after all your...kindness when I was wounded."

"I pressed thee too much, intruded on thy private sorrow about the war. I apologize to thee. Meddling is a sin, too."

He chuckled suddenly. "You? Meddle? Never."

She laughed, too. "Oh, a direct hit."

"You're not letting that incident…about Tarver's window get to you?" His self-protection alarm was clanging. He needed to get away from this woman who somehow always stripped him of his mask.

"It hurt," she said simply.

Missy came out. "Dr. Mercy, I know which peppermint candy I want."

Welcoming this chance to retreat from the field, Lon tipped his hat and hurried away.

The cloudy day did nothing to still his restlessness. He walked faster. Part of him wanted to grab his valise and set out west for Boise and maybe farther. But he found himself bound to Idaho Bend.

At night, he'd been gambling and winning, but he'd begun to hate the saloon—the drunken behavior, the raucous laughter, everything he used to enjoy. Then another upsetting thought hit him.

Who had scrawled those awful words on the store window?

Lon wanted to put his fist into someone's face. Now his stride lagged—he found he couldn't go on. He was still weak from his stab wound and the subsequent fever. He closed his eyes a moment, then turned back to the saloon where he needed to rest until evening. Forced to walk slower, Lon glowered at the sleepy Main Street and lonely sky. Maybe it was time to move on. Yet he couldn't force Mercy Gabriel's face from his mind. He knew she was the anchor that tethered him here. And that must end. Soon.

Evening had come. Mercy watched Indigo setting a new red-and-white-checked oilcloth on the table. It was pretty and gave the humble cabin a festive appearance. This, along with a morning spent in Missy's lively company and the setting in motion of Mercy's plans for better public heath, should have revived her spirits. But it was her meeting with Lon that had truly lifted her up. She had been surprised by his honest apology and heartfelt thanks, and she'd spent the rest of the day fighting the urge to smile constantly. She was trying very hard not to think about what it all meant.

"I've been meaning to tell you," Indigo said with her back to Mercy, "that I've invited someone to eat with us this evening."

Mercy inhaled. Was Indigo finally ready to share with her the man she'd become interested in? Would he be suitable or dangerous to Indigo's reputation? Mercy plunged ahead. "Is he the young man I've seen thee talking to?"

Indigo turned and grinned. "You miss nothing, Aunt Mercy."

Neither does Ma Bailey. Any kind of gossip could make Indigo the target of… Mercy didn't want to put it into words. But a certain kind of man would take advantage of any woman deemed less than respectable. And it could tinge the standing of Mercy's fledgling medical practice. Mercy closed her eyes, resisting the temptation to worry.

Indigo began singing to herself, "There'll be peace in the valley for me someday, I pray no more sorrow and sadness or trouble will be, there'll be peace in the valley for me, there the flowers will be blooming, the grass will be green…"

Listening to Indigo's low, sweet voice, Mercy turned her thoughts back to the present. *No use borrowing trouble.* "I certainly haven't missed seeing how this young man has succeeded in bringing out thy smiles and laughter," Mercy said, feeling guilty over her reservations. *Lord, let me be wrong.*

"He does make me laugh," Indigo replied as she began to set the table for three.

"Then he must be a good man."

"At first I tried to avoid him," Indigo said. "I mean, I am a woman of color and he's part white. But he says his mother won't care."

"He has a mother living?" Mercy asked.

"Yes, farther north, near Canada. He came down to see if he could make some money mining or logging."

"And what is this young man's name?" Mercy watched Indigo trying to hide how much joy merely speaking of her beau gave her.

"He is Pierre Gauthier."

The names sounded good together. "I will, of course, make him welcome. What are thee preparing this evening?" Mercy glanced at the covered cast-iron pot hanging over the fire, gently humming with steam.

"Pierre went hunting and brought the meat over earlier. So I put it to roast with some wild onions and a few potatoes. I'm baking a pie, too." Indigo pointed to the covered Dutch oven on a trivet sitting in the back of the fire. "I picked some late berries this afternoon. One of the miners eating at the café told me where to look for them. Wasn't that nice?"

Mercy nodded her agreement. "Sounds like a lovely meal." *I hope Pierre Gauthier is worthy of it.*

A jaunty knock sounded on the door.

"That's him." Indigo's face lit up like a lightning bug. She hurried to the door and opened it.

"Bonjour, ma jeune fille."

The man spoke French?

He walked inside, carrying a basket of fall leaves and pinecones. "I thought you might dress up your cabin with these."

Mercy couldn't help herself—she was impressed. "What a lovely gift."

He strode to her and executed a bow. "I am Pierre Gauthier, Dr. Gabriel."

She gave him her hand. "Welcome to our home, Pierre Gauthier."

"Merci, Docteur."

Another knock on the door sounded. Mercy glanced at Indigo who shrugged and went to the door.

"Hello, Indigo. I've come to speak to Dr. Gabriel."

Lon? Mercy was caught completely off guard.

Indigo looked back at her. "Please come in, Mr. Mackey."

Lon entered, doffing his hat. Then he paused, obviously surprised to see Pierre. His face changed in a moment from the honest one he had worn when they had spoken together earlier to the gambler's cool veneer.

Lon nodded toward Pierre. "I'm so sorry to intrude. I didn't know you had company."

"Lon—" Mercy began, but couldn't finish her sentence. How did she say, *Don't act like this?*

"You must come in, sir," Indigo said, managing to take his hat from his hand. "We were just about to sit down to supper and we have more than enough for four."

Lon looked ready to decline. And Mercy felt her former good spirits vanishing.

"*Mon ami,* stay," Pierre said expansively. "You will even up the numbers." He grinned. "Two ladies and two gentlemen."

Mercy lifted her tight lips into a smile. Having another man at the table might give her a better perspective of this young man. If only Lon wouldn't carry on his "I am just a carefree gambler" role. "Yes, Lon Mackey, please stay."

"As you wish, Doctor," he said archly.

Soon the men sat on the bench on one side of the table. "Mademoiselle Indigo, something smells delicious," Pierre said.

Indigo beamed and turned toward the fire.

"Thee are French, Pierre Gauthier?" Mercy asked, trying to relieve the tense atmosphere in the small cabin.

"Please, call me Pierre. And I am Métis."

Mercy didn't want to seem rude, but the words popped out. "What is that?"

"It's the name given to Indians who intermarried with the French fur traders much earlier, before the U.S. was even a nation," Lon said smoothly.

"*Oui,* I am French and Ojibwa and Dakota Sioux also. Most Métis live in Canada, but my family settled on this side of the border."

"Ah." That explained the mix of French in his English and the blend of races in his face and build.

Lon looked pained with the polite conversation. Or was it something else?

"Indigo says thee has a mother," she said, forging on.

Pierre nodded. "Mackey, do you not gamble tonight?"

Lon cleared his throat. "I will be in the saloon tonight if you should wish to try your luck with the cards." His mouth quirked into a faint smirk.

In spite of Lon's provocation, Mercy kept her face impassive. *Lon, I won't let thee lure me into any discussion of thy gambling.* She hated that their new accord was slipping through her fingers.

"I was stopping to let Dr. Gabriel," Lon said,

watching her, "know that I intend to leave town in the next few days. Since our paths rarely cross except in passing, I didn't want her to find out secondhand."

Mercy's insides turned over. "Thee plan on leaving?"

Indigo stopped on her way to the table. "Leaving? Why?"

Lon shrugged. "Gamblers never stay in one place for long. Miss Indigo, that certainly does smell delicious."

Indigo set the meal on the table and began serving. Lon lifted an eyebrow, his expression almost a challenge to Mercy.

Mercy tried to keep up the conversation while trying to decide why Lon had come and if he was sincere in planning to leave.

An hour after the meal, Pierre excused himself. "I must go home and sleep. I begin work at dawn." He bid Mercy a formal goodnight and then lifted Indigo's hand, kissed it, and left, murmuring, *"Bon nuit, ma chère,"* before he left.

Lon had not followed the young Métis out. He rose. "I thank you, ladies, for an excellent meal. But I must go earn my living at the saloon. I will need sufficient funds to leave town."

"Is thee really leaving town?" Mercy asked, unable to stop herself.

"Indeed. I hope to leave by week's end." He bowed, donned his hat and departed.

Indigo closed the door and then leaned back

against it. She straightened, looking directly into Mercy's eyes. "What do you think of Pierre, Aunt Mercy?"

Mercy tried to sort through all her impressions, but Lon's unexpected announcement had distracted her. "I like him," she said at last. "I don't know how anyone could not like him."

"But you don't think that's good enough." Indigo's face looked downcast.

"I didn't say that." Mercy had no room to talk. She knew by now that Lon commanded her attention more than he should. She also tried to think of a way to ask the question that had not been asked.

"You're wondering if he's friends with the Lord?"

Mercy walked to Indigo and put an arm around her. Lon did not appear to be friends with the Lord. War could do that to any man. But when her daughter didn't answer the question, Mercy's smile slipped away. *Oh, dear.*

"I don't know the answer to that, Aunt Mercy."

Mercy gazed at Indigo's lovely face. So young, so pretty, so wanting to be loved. "We will pray about it."

"But I am going to have to ask him, right?" Indigo looked as if she were hoping Mercy would say no.

Mercy nodded. "Thee *must* know the answer."

Sudden tears sprang into Indigo's eyes. "I don't want to lose him."

Lon Mackey slipped into Mercy's mind, and

her mind repeated Indigo's words, *I don't want to lose him.*

How can I lose what I never had? Yet Lon Mackey was the only man who had ever lingered in her mind like this. This left her feeling empty. If Lon left town, would every day fill her with this sense of loneliness and loss?

It had taken a bit longer than Mercy had hoped to get the meeting arranged at the church where she and Indigo had treated the last few cholera patients. Nonetheless, today, humming with anticipation and nervousness, Mercy walked to the front of the church. She looked out over the small gathering of around thirty women all dressed in their Sunday best. Would they listen with understanding to what she had to say? Or would they reject what she longed to teach them?

"Good afternoon, ladies. I'm so glad that thee has come to hear about some of the discoveries doctors here and abroad have been making about the human body and how to keep it healthy."

Ma Bailey sat front and center, glaring at Mercy.

Mercy resisted the temptation to lift her chin. However, if Ma Bailey thought she could take this hopeful beginning and turn it to dust, she was mistaken.

"The recent cholera epidemic is an example of a disease that can be stopped with public sanitation."

"What's public sanitation?" Ma Bailey snapped.

"Public sanitation is the name of the emerging

movement to keep people healthy through clean water and food." Mercy forged on, preempting Ma Bailey, who was trying to be heard. "As early as the 1830s, New York State passed laws to keep their water sources free of contamination from animal carcasses."

As Ma Bailey opened her mouth again, Mercy hurried on. "Here, the first family to succumb to the cholera was the family that had made and brought the berry juice to the church meeting. Subsequently, dead rats were found in their well."

A communal gasp went through the women. "No one told us that," Ellen Dunfield declared, an angry edge to her voice.

Mercy nodded. "Thee may ask Lon Mackey and the bartender, Tom Banks. They discovered the rats themselves."

This revelation was followed by a buzz of upset voices. Mercy hoped she had as good a poker face as any gambler because inside, she was rejoicing. The truth was a powerful force.

Mercy was about to go on when the door at the back of the church opened slowly. In the shaft of sunlight, Mercy couldn't see who had come late. Her eyes adjusted, and she saw Chen Park and his wife standing just inside the church. *Father in heaven, I never expected them to come. Help them be welcomed, not shunned.* "Chen Park and Chen An," she greeted them as she went up the aisle.

Both of them bowed low several times. The

husband spoke, "We hear you tell women how to keep babies well."

"Yes, I'm speaking on how to keep babies healthy. Please take a seat." She motioned toward the nearest pew, which was far behind the nearest woman. Mercy hated the separation, but realized that this was neither the time nor the place for a lesson on the evils of discrimination.

The Chinese couple made their way into the pew and sat down. Mercy walked back to the front, ignoring the low rush of disapproving voices discussing the arrival of the Chens. She heard Ma Bailey hiss, "Heathens in a church."

Before Mercy could reply, another woman said, "Mrs. Bailey, there will be every tribe and nation in heaven."

To stem this theological debate, Mercy began speaking again. "Now many of thee have known women who have lost children due to milk fever."

At these words, an anxious silence fell on the assembled parents. Milk fever killed many infants each year in the warm months. "Thee should know," Mercy continued, "that a scientist named Louis Pasteur has shown that boiling milk destroys bacteria. And bacteria are what carry disease."

"Bacteria?" Ellen echoed.

"Yes, as early as the 1600s a Dutchman, Antonie van Leeuwenhoek, developed lenses that could see living bacteria, which is too small for the human eye to see—"

"If it's too small for us to see, how did that ol' Dutchman see it then? Answer me that," Ma Bailey crowed.

Mercy held her temper, which wanted to break away from her like a racehorse. Did this woman never have a helpful thought?

"Thee has seen spectacles, hasn't thee? Antonie van Leeuwenhoek ground glass lenses finer and finer, and as he did, he saw more. Pasteur used the microscope that Leeuwenhoek developed with finely ground lenses to view bacteria and their effects."

Ma Bailey scowled.

"These bacteria are what make us sick?" another woman asked with a shyly raised hand as if she were in school.

"That is what scientists think. They are studying how bacteria do this, but we all know that contact with a sick person or even their clothing and bedding can spread a disease."

"That's right," Ellen agreed.

"Well, what do these scientists have to do with what we're doin' in the Idaho Territory?" Ma Bailey demanded.

"Very simply, some scientists have had good results after boiling questionable water and milk. So if—"

The pastor of the church ran inside, startling Mercy and the ladies. He halted at the pull rope and began tolling the bell. "Mine cave-in!" he shouted.

The women leaped to their feet, some with a

shriek. Mercy's audience fled down the center aisle and outside. The pastor continued to yank on the bell rope. The steeple bell joined what sounded like the fire bell, bellowing on Main Street, calling for help.

The frantic tolling blasted through Mercy like gunpowder. She had read once in a newspaper that a woman had confessed to being "drenched with terror." Now Mercy knew exactly how that felt. The familiar twin jolt of energy and alarm rushed through her, the same jolt that had come whenever a cannon had roared.

She rushed from the church and over to her office to gather up supplies she might need for victims of a cave-in. Instead of wounds caused by grapeshot and lead bullets, she would no doubt be faced with the aftermath of bodies crushed or struck by falling rock and wood supports.

Like a bee straight to its hive, a sudden thought whizzed through her. Pierre Gauthier was a miner. *Father, protect this fine young man. Indigo's heart would be broken if anything happened to him.*

Chapter Seven

Lon stood, looking over the still-swinging doors of the saloon. He watched the town race like a pack of rats up the street toward the mountainside. He fought the urge to grab his hat and join the exodus. He gripped the top of the doors and stopped them from rattling. Or tried. Not only did he hear the pounding footsteps pelting down the wooden sidewalk in front, but the sound also communicated through the wood vibrating in his hands.

He released the doors and turned away. As he did, he saw Mercy. He cursed himself for his weakness in continuing to think of her as "Mercy." He saw that she was hurrying along with the others, her black bag in her hand, racing to the rescue. Lon turned away, resisting the urge to follow her.

He recalled that recent evening when he'd ended up going to her cabin. Why had he felt the need to tell her he intended to leave? Had he somehow hoped she'd try to talk him out of going? While she hadn't, her startled-wide eyes at his announcement had haunted him ever since. *But I'm right. This town is bad news.*

Would the Quaker never learn to watch out for herself first? Had she already forgotten that after saving countless lives from cholera, this town had handed her less than five bucks for her tireless efforts? Had she already forgotten that no one in this town would rent her a room because she had adopted a Negro orphan in the war? His gut burned with the injustice. *Well, perhaps St. Mercy can forget, but I won't.*

Mercy arrived at the mine as angry gray clouds scudded fast and free overhead. In the milling crowd, she tried to decide whom to approach. Who was in charge? Who would *take* charge?

Mercy began looking around and then realized she was seeking Lon. For all she knew, Lon was already gone. That thought gave her the familiar empty, lonely feeling.

Even standing on her tiptoes, she couldn't see a leader of the rescue effort. If only she were taller, or she'd been a tomboy, like her sister, Felicity. If Felicity were here, she'd climb a tree to get a bird's-eye view of the crowd.

Then Mercy glimpsed a tall man with red hair. It was Digger Hobson, the mining company manager. She began threading her way through the crowd, which was becoming larger and larger by the minute. As she ventured toward the man, the throng surrounding him became tighter and tighter. She was soon forced to beg men to give way to her. They did, of course. Even though she was an odd woman, she was still a woman and must be treated with deference.

"Digger Hobson," she said, arriving at his side, panting. "How serious is it? Are men trapped?"

Amid all the other voices clamoring for information or giving advice, he glanced down at her. "I'm glad you're here."

His simple, direct words were both welcome and unwelcome. If he were glad to see her, it must be gravely serious. Heart throbbing, she drew in a calming breath. "Has the rescue effort begun?" she asked.

During this exchange, the men around him had quieted, listening. Raising both hands, Digger spoke in a strong, ringing voice, "We're trying to figure out what exactly has happened. There are some men inside assessing the situation."

"Have there been cave-ins here before? Does thee have experience in recovering miners alive?" she asked. At her questions, more and more people fell silent around them.

"I've been in mining most of my life, so, yes, I have experience." Digger gave her a grim look. "We've had a few minor cave-ins, but this sounded bigger to my ears."

His words hung in the air over them all. "I will stay as long as I am needed," she said.

He reached for her hand and gripped it momentarily. "If you weren't here, we'd have to transport any injured a day's journey to Boise. So thank you."

Mercy's insides clenched, thinking of injured men lying on buckboards, being rattled over bumpy trails and getting reinjured on that rough trip. Some would die from the journey itself.

From the mine entrance, a younger man came forward, shoving his way to Digger Hobson. "The rescue party is ready, Monsieur Digger. We have filled already our oil lanterns. The equipment, it is ready, and we have the new beams to hold up the unstable walls. You must only give the word."

Mercy was relieved to recognize the young man as Pierre Gauthier. She learned much about him in that moment. He was at the forefront of the rescue effort, which meant Digger Hobson trusted him. And Pierre Gauthier was concerned—very concerned— for others. Indigo had chosen well.

Digger nodded to Pierre, then raised his hands and his voice again, saying, "The crew has cleared away the loose debris. Now they're going to work their way into the mine. They have to move slow so they don't set off another cave-in. Everyone should fall back so we can maneuver—"

"Please!" Ellen Dunfield called out from where she stood with the other miners' wives. "Please, we need to know who's in the mine." The women around Ellen added their voices in agreement.

Digger Hobson frowned. "If you don't see them here, they're probably in the cave-in." Many of the women gasped in unison. "Now everyone fall back and open paths for my men to work."

"I'll stay with the women until I'm needed," Mercy declared, mustering all her strength and will. She headed straight for Ellen. She took Ellen's small, cold hand in hers and led her away from the workers. And as if she were the leader, most of the women followed her. She led them higher on the nearby slope so that they would be able to see yet not be in the way.

"We must not give in to fear," Mercy declared. "'God is our refuge and strength, a very present help in trouble,'" she quoted. Spontaneously, all the women joined hands and bowed their heads.

"Please pray for us, Dr. Mercy," Ellen said, her brave voice quavering.

The anxiety mounting all around Mercy pulled at her, weighing her down. Still, in this request, she discerned the silent pleading for reassurance and hope. She took a deep breath and prayed aloud, "Father, we need Thy mercy and provision. Loved ones may be in the mine. We ask that Thy presence enfold them, that help will be able to reach them in time. Help us pray as we ought to." Then she began the Lord's Prayer and the women all joined in.

When Mercy looked up, tears still streamed down the women's faces. But they had all drawn together.

They had put this awful occurrence into God's hands. They would face this together.

Then the waiting began. Strong winds from the southwest buffeted them, making Mercy tie her bonnet ribbons tighter. The racing clouds darkened. They became a moving gray-flannel roof over each head. And, below, the gloom of fear hovered over each heart. How long would it take the rescuers to reach the trapped men, the husbands and fathers who loved and protected them?

Lon stood alone in the dim, shuttered saloon. After hours of no customers, even the bartender had been unable to resist the call of the mine cave-in. Alone, hands in his pockets, Lon walked to his bunk in the back room. He sat on it and stared at the blank wall. It was time to start packing—Idaho Bend was not working out for him. First had come the cholera, then being stabbed nearly to death and now a cave-in. It was time to move on to a luckier place. He pulled his valise toward him. His belongings were sparse. His hand touched his father's gold pocket watch and his mother's locket. He held one in each hand. Who could have predicted that they would die while he was away, facing bullets, sabers and grapeshot? *Mother would have liked Mercy.* He crushed this errant thought and thrust the two mementos back into the pouch where they belonged. Maybe going all the way to the Pacific would be a good change for him. Mercy Gabriel was claiming too much of his mind.

* * *

Near evening, Indigo led the children she had been watching during the church meeting to the mine site. They walked hand in hand up the last few feet toward the women around Mercy. The children ran to their mothers, who folded them into their arms. A sudden harsh gust of wind grabbed their skirt hems, twirling them. Some mothers lost their bonnets to the wind and their children chased and caught them.

Mercy overheard children asking about fathers and uncles and older brothers, and mothers soothing them. The wind snatched at their voices, carrying them far. But Mercy's heart ached for these little ones. They could barely understand anything, except that something bad had happened in the mine and that something more dreadful might come.

"I kept them away from here as long as I could," Indigo murmured into Mercy's ear, "but they need supper."

Mercy took Indigo's hand in hers. "Pierre is helping with the rescue effort."

"You saw him?" Indigo's eyes revealed the strain of unspoken worry.

Mercy nodded and squeezed Indigo's hand. She knew the longer it took to reach the trapped miners, the less hope there would be for survivors. The rescuers were also in danger of subsequent cave-ins. Closing her eyes, she grappled with this hard fact. She opened her eyes, refusing to give in to the despair that clutched at her spirit like icy fingers.

She faced the women. "If thee must go home to care for and feed thy children, go. Indigo and I will stay, and she will bring word to thee if any progress is made." *Or if thy loved one is pulled from the mine— living or dead.* She didn't need to say this out loud. Why should she? It was what they all were thinking, fearing.

Blinking rapidly, Ellen Dunfield swallowed down obvious tears. "Thank you, Dr. Mercy. The children must be taken home for some care and comfort. It's best for them."

Mercy appreciated this young woman's quick response and the assurance it brought to the rest of the waiting women. Ellen lifted her son into her arms and took Missy's hand in hers. Together they started down the rise toward town. Soon only women without children remained on the hillside.

Mercy noticed that several older men were starting a fire at the mine entrance. Even protected as it was from the wild wind, the blaze sent sparks flying high on the relentless gusts.

Ma Bailey came into sight around the bend, walking between the shafts of a two-wheeled cart, dragging it behind her. From the cart, the wind carried the scents of biscuits, bacon and something sweet. Ma stopped by Digger. "I made biscuits and fried bacon, Mr. Hobson, for the men working to open the mine. And I'd already baked cinnamon rolls for tomorrow's breakfast."

Mercy waited to hear what the tightfisted

woman would be charging for this needed and welcome food.

"It's free," Ma barked as if arguing with someone unseen, "to the workers."

Mercy stood, astounded. The wind took advantage of her distraction and untied her bonnet ribbons. She caught the bonnet just before it sailed away.

"I just hope no one comes out dead," Ma said, looking mournful.

Mercy wished Ma Bailey hadn't added this, but she couldn't find fault with this cantankerous woman today.

Indigo spoke up, "I have food I can bring, too. I baked bread last night. I'll go home and get it." Several other women hurried along with Indigo, calling that they would be back soon with more food and drink for the vigil.

The older men continued to tend the fire at the mine entrance. A few held spades, ready to put out any sparks that might escape and ignite the grass. The orange flames were welcome against the graying sky and the chill from the damp ground.

Suddenly, Mercy missed Lon Mackey. Had the whole town come out to work together—even ill-natured, stingy Ma Bailey—while he had stayed behind? Could it be that he was truly gone already? *Lon Mackey, if thee is still here, thee must come. Thee will never forgive thyself if men die and thee did nothing. Thee may deny that, but I know thee better.*

* * *

The long evening stretched into a long night, and the rushing wind brought the scent of rain. Mercy wrapped her shawl more tightly around herself. Men kept working, digging through the blocked mine shaft. The sound of their picks and shovels could be heard even above the surging wind. The men took turns coming out periodically to warm their hands by the fire, drink strong coffee and swallow any food handed to them.

The mothers had returned with their children. They had tucked them, wrapped in blankets and quilts, into mining wagons to sleep together, to comfort one another. It was touching to see little children patting each other and talking softly.

In light of the coming storm, large canvas sheets had been set up and lashed over the wagons, making snug tents. Mercy and the mothers clutched shawls around themselves and paced around the fire, shivering and praying.

Distant thunder sounded against the stiff wind, stirring the night. She found herself glancing at the mining shack where the rescuers would take anyone they carried out. And then her gaze would return to the fire at the mine entrance. There lantern lights flickered as men went in and out.

The impetuous, worrisome storm rushed toward them—closer, closer. Over the western mountains, lightning flickered ominously. Which would come first—survivors from the mine or the big storm bearing down on them? Finally worn out, she leaned back against one of the wagons filled with sleeping children.

"Mercy."

She jerked upright. Lon was standing beside her. He had come. Golden joy surged within her spirit. She threw her arms around him, so solid, stalwart—so welcome.

Bright lightning splintered overhead.

Sudden thunder hammered like a blacksmith working iron.

By the crackling lightning, she glimpsed two men carrying a miner from the cavelike entrance. She ran toward them, Lon's hand in hers. Lon jogged beside her, trying to make himself heard. Mercy couldn't understand what Lon was shouting in her ear, but there was no time to stop. The brunt of the violent storm had reached them.

Lightning flashed quick and steady like the tapping of a telegraph key. Cold rain poured down on them, snatching Mercy's breath. Thunder pounded, battered them. Jagged lightning streaked, struck and ignited.

The cold rain had soaked Lon in a moment.

Struck by lightning, a nearby tall pine exploded, flinging branches, pine needles and flaming sparks over them. Mercy ducked as Lon threw his arm around her shoulders to protect her.

When they reached the men with the stretcher, one

of them shouted into Lon's ear, but Lon couldn't hear the words over the thunder. Then another two men came out carrying a man by the shoulders and feet. Mercy waved the men toward the mining shack. Lon continued into the mine. Maybe he hadn't delayed too long, maybe he had come at the right time to help support the injured as they staggered out.

Thunder continued, blasting overhead like an artillery barrage. The sound battered him physically, shook him until his teeth rattled. Then an explosion like a cannon shell threw him to the mud.

Panic. He yelled, his voice vanishing into the maelstrom. Rocks cascaded down the slopes around them. Some bounced high, barreling into the valley where he lay facedown. He covered his head with his arms. Squeezed his eyes shut. And prayed.

At last the earth ceased vibrating. He opened his eyes and sucked in air. He was alive. He hadn't been snatched up in the whirlwind. Pushing up with both hands, he got to his feet. He staggered and caught himself.

The storm was already past them, moving east. Yet the flashing lightning still illuminated the surroundings. And thunder boomed so close, too close. When he looked to the mine, he gasped, shock rippling through him. An avalanche of rocks had fallen, blocking the entrance. *Dear God, help.*

He glanced around for Mercy. Was she out of harm's way? He saw an oil lamp shining dimly through the mine shack window, illuminating her silhouette. She was safe.

Soon he was surrounded by the few men left and several women. He couldn't tell if it was rain or tears streaming down their faces. They all looked to him, beseeching him to tell them what to do.

The urge to turn tail and run hit him like a blast of buckshot. But one glance at their faces and he was powerless to desert them. "Form lines!" he shouted against the receding yet still roaring thunder. "Like bucket brigades! Start moving out rock! If it's too big to lift, roll it!"

He ran forward and they followed. He hefted a large rock and then started it down the line. Two more lines formed. The horror of what had just happened twisted inside him like the tightening of a screw. The rescuers had been swallowed up by the avalanche, along with Digger, the mine manager.

Even as the work began, he despaired. There weren't enough rescuers. Too many had been swallowed by the mine. How many would they find still alive?

The rocks cut his soft gambler palms, gouged his knuckles. If only there were more hands. Then he saw movement by the light of the retreating storm. Suddenly, another line formed beside his. Who was it?

Then he saw—the Chinese had come to help. The men formed another line and began moving rock away from the blocked entrance. He didn't know why they'd come to help. But he was humbly grateful. Choked up, he couldn't utter even a word of welcome.

The rock brigades worked steady and determined for hours. The storm finally moved beyond their valley, no doubt still spreading destruction eastward. Lon's arms and back ached. The black night wrapped around them. Drenched, Lon shivered in the cold. He gasped for air.

Occasionally a man would grunt; a woman would moan. Someone was praying aloud—the Twenty-third Psalm. The phrase "the valley of the shadow of death" repeated in his mind. *Lord, bring the sunrise. Let some live.*

Mercy had never passed a more terrifying night. First the cave-in, then the storm, terrifying in its destruction. Rampaging thunder. Lightning exploding and flaming about. Then rocks pouring down, shattering, crashing, smothering.

In the mining shack, she stood, looking out the one small window into the murky gray of predawn and an early mist. Her arms were folded as if holding back a well of shock and distress. Was Lon still out there working? She didn't know and couldn't leave her patients to find out.

A moan sounded behind her. She turned to one of her two patients lying on the earthen floor and took his pulse. She hadn't been able to do much for either of them. She had managed to clean the area around their gashes and stop the bleeding.

But if they had sustained internal injuries, there was nothing she could do.

A knock sounded on the door. Indigo rose from the floor and opened it. The pastor of the church where Mercy had been speaking just hours before peered in.

"We haven't spoken directly, but I'm Pastor Stephen Willis. My wife and I have prepared the church for the injured."

"Thank You, Jesus," Indigo murmured. Mercy repeated the words silently.

"The wagon is all ready to take the injured there," he said.

Mercy looked at her two patients, who took up almost all the floor space. Only these two had been brought out of the mine before the storm and avalanche. How many remained trapped? How many remained alive? Tears clogged her throat.

Indigo must have sensed this. She responded for Mercy, "We just have these two so far, Pastor. I'll help you carry them to the wagon."

Mercy wished she could give in to the tears that crouched just behind her eyes. However, she knew intuitively that any show of emotion on her part would weaken her reputation as a physician. Male doctors showed little emotion—she must do the same or be dismissed as just an emotional female.

She sighed and put her bonnet on again. She prayed for the men still trapped in the mine as she went out into the chill, damp fog that misted her face.

She glanced at the lines of people ferrying rock away from the mine entrance. Ma Bailey had somehow got a fire started in spite of the heavy soaking they'd received. She was giving mugs of steaming coffee to tired workers.

Then the fog lifted; Mercy halted. She looked more closely toward one line passing rock away from the avalanche. The Chinese men were working along with the Americans. Praise for God flowed through her. How touching that these unwanted strangers in this land were willing to help in this time of disaster. And she hadn't imagined Lon arriving, or the feel of his arm protecting her. A few times last night she'd doubted her memory. Lon was still there, directing the rescue. He had come late, but he had come.

Mercy hurried to Lon. He broke away from the brigade and took her hands in his. "Mercy, where are you taking the injured?"

She felt the roughness of his hands. "Pastor Willis has opened his church as a hospital." She wished she had time to treat his lacerated hands.

"The progress is slow." He wiped his grimy, damp forehead with his sleeve. Once again, Lon's flashy gambler clothing clashed with the man and his actions in a crisis. *Thee may try to make thyself and everyone else believe thee wants to live as a gambler, Lon Mackey. Thee will never make me believe it.*

"How are thee faring?" she asked, leaning close to catch his low voice.

He squeezed her hands in reply. Someone called to him. "Take care," he said as he rushed off.

"And thee!" she called after him, missing his touch immediately. A spark of warmth flared within— hope.

Lon glanced over his shoulder, watching Mercy and Indigo mounting a buckboard. A man with a clerical collar was helping them up. He wished he could call her back. Her presence always lent strength. But another woman already sat in the wagon bed, obviously to help Mercy. Two pairs of feet protruded from the end of the wagon bed. They must be taking the two victims of the cave-in to town. Were they being taken for treatment or burial?

Death. Death was their real enemy, their constant adversary, always ready to suck out their breath and put them in the ground.

A shout sounded. Lon turned.

"We're through!" one of the miners yelled.

Lon hurried to the hole they had finally cleared through the rock barrier. "Let's be careful. We need to widen this opening and get a rescuer who will fit through it."

One of the Chinese waved and bowed. "I can go through." Lon blinked away deep emotion that was trying to surface. These immigrants were barely deemed human by many of the miners they were offering to save. Their willingness to help was humbling.

"Thanks," Lon said, returning the bow.

The Chinese man said, "I Chen Park. Woman doctor bring my baby."

Lon nodded. "Dr. Mercy Gabriel is a good doctor." *A good woman. Too good for this bunch.*

"Yes." Chen Park said. "Dr. Mercy. Good."

Lon noticed that everyone else had fallen silent, watching this exchange.

"Thank God Dr. Gabriel came to town when she did," said Ellen Dunfield. "If she hadn't, many of us would already be in the grave." She glanced over her shoulder toward the wagons where the children were still sleeping. Then she sank to the ground, exhausted from hours of nonstop labor.

"Is this hole big enough?" the miner closest to the opening asked.

"Big enough for me." Chen Park hurried forward and accepted a lantern. "I go in."

The other miners called out encouragement, "Good man! God bless!"

The man ducked low and entered the hole.

Lon could only hope that this brave man would be able to reach someone alive—and stay alive himself.

Chapter Eight

The watery morning sun had finally burned away the fog. Lon passed another rock down the line. His back felt broken; his arm muscles trembled. He was so exhausted he could have sunk to the ground and fallen instantly into a deep sleep. But each labored breath reminded him that men trapped inside might have little chance to go on breathing if the rescuers didn't work faster—if they didn't reach them in time. The old feelings that had plagued him before each battle—the cramping in his stomach, the tautness in his neck—flared to life. He would have no ease until all were accounted for—living and dead.

The Chinese men were taking turns going into the hole, carrying or rolling out large rocks to make room for the injured to pass through. But the progress only inched forward. Lon fought his impatience.

Then Chen Park returned, grinning. "I see men. Touch men."

"It must be the rescue party," Lon said, gasping, his breathing shallow and his pulse suddenly racing. "They rushed in and were caught by the avalanche."

"Three—" he held up three fingers "—under rocks." He shook his head. "Not breathe. Four still breathe but sleep." The news horrified but invigorated the men and women still moving rock. Close, so close. Lon and the rest who were still able to work began frantically widening the hole.

Lon passed rock after rock, straining with their weight. His whole body ached and he often found his eyes shutting. But he was used to pushing himself beyond the limits of his strength. The women who had worked all night staggered away to care for their waking children.

Panting and wheezing, some of the older men fell where they stood in line. Younger men carried them near the fire and covered them with blankets. Everyone's willingness to work until they dropped stoked a flame in Lon's heart. *We'll save some. God help us.*

Chen Park came out backward, gasping, obviously laboring hard. He was pulling a man. Lon hurried forward to help along with the other workers. He could see Digger Hobson's red hair. Hands grabbed Digger and helped carry him out. An incredible rush of energy charged Lon. He saw it reflected in the grinning faces around him. They had broken through. Finally.

"Chen Park," Lon said, "well done. Thanks."

The man bowed low. "Hole big enough for bigger men to go in." He wiped sweat from his forehead. "Hole bigger inside."

Then Lon noticed Digger's right foot. His boot looked crushed. Chen Park nodded. "Foot under rock. Bad."

Lon squeezed Chen's shoulder. "You did your best. You need to rest. You men have been carrying the brunt since early morning. Rest."

Chen nodded and motioned toward his fellows. "We go home. Eat. Come back."

"Thanks," Lon said again, his voice low and gravelly. He didn't want them to stop, yet they were only flesh and blood.

The Chinese men walked away, stretching their backs and rotating their tired shoulders. The women and children waved and called out their thanks.

Pastor Willis, who had been waiting for survivors, drove the wagon close to the mine. Lon turned his attention to another survivor who had just been brought out. It was that young Métis he'd played poker with and later met at Mercy's, the one who was sweet on Indigo. He was still unconscious.

Men helped Pastor Willis load both injured miners into the wagon, and he drove away. Then more men were carried out, but they were dead. The rescuers covered them with wool blankets as women knelt beside them and mourned.

Let down after the brief elation, Lon turned away. The cries of the women shredded his heart. *At least during the war, I didn't have to hear the widows mourning.* But he'd had to write letters to them, telling them of their husbands' last days and how they had died. He rubbed his chest over his heart, trying to banish the physical pain these memories always caused him. Here and now, however, he had not given the order sending these men into the mine. This had not happened under his command.

He stood very still, drawing up, hauling up all his reserves of strength. They had one more barrier to break through to reach the men who'd been trapped in the original cave-in. Once again, every eye had turned toward him, asking for direction, encouragement. Why was everyone here depending on him? He had no answer. But then he was depending on Dr. Mercy to save as many survivors as she could. Yet he knew that even she couldn't save everyone, either.

At the church hospital, Mercy looked with dismay at Digger Hobson. He had just regained consciousness and was writhing with what must be unbearable pain.

A long, rectangular table had been brought from the saloon and set up where the pulpit usually stood. Mercy directed the men to carry Digger and lay him on it. She must perform surgery on him as soon as possible. His foot was crushed and might soon become gangrenous, which could kill this good man.

Mercy looked around and saw that they had carried

in another patient. As soon as she heard Indigo's outcry, she knew it must be Pierre. She hurried to Indigo and lifted Pierre's wrist. "His pulse is slow but steady," she said. But she didn't like the look of his bruised and bloodied head. Mercy ran her hands over him, checking for other injuries. His right arm was broken.

She looked to Indigo, feeling the sting of her daughter's pain as her own. "He is not in immediate danger. We must treat Digger Hobson first."

Her lips trembling, Indigo looked into Mercy's eyes and said quietly, bravely, "I'll prepare for surgery."

Mercy squeezed Indigo's shoulder and then went to prepare herself for this ordeal. Dread opened inside her, sucking away her composure. She hated what she must do. She had assisted in so many amputations during the war that she'd already known how to perform one before she started medical school. But that didn't lessen her loathing of them.

Soon, she stood wearing a clean, white apron. She looked down at her gleaming surgical instruments, which Indigo had laid out for her on spotless cotton. Mercy took up the scalpel. Indigo was administering ether from a sponge and Digger had just become unconscious. The familiar rush of energy and clarity sharpened her mind and bolstered her will to do this thing.

About halfway through the operation, someone came into the church and demanded, "What's going on here?" Heavy footsteps hurried up behind Mercy. The same voice challenged her, "Good grief, woman, what are you thinking? You can't do an amputation!"

Mercy didn't, couldn't pause in her surgery. "I'm very sorry, but I must ask thee to step away. I am at a very delicate part of the operation and cannot allow any distractions." From the corner of her eye, she glimpsed an older man.

"You stop that right now. I'll take over. I'm a qualified physician. No nurse is up to this kind of surgery."

"I, too, am a qualified physician," Mercy said, keeping her main focus on the operation.

He grabbed her arm.

Wild outrage shot through Mercy. Digger's life hung in the balance. "Get this man off me!" she called out. "He's keeping me from my work! Digger could die!"

A number of women hurried over. "Let go of Dr. Mercy. She's right in the middle—"

Hot words boiled out of the man, and he did not release Mercy's arm.

So Mercy did something she had never done before. She kicked the man's shin as hard as she could and swung her hip at him, knocking him off balance. Releasing his grip, he fell, shouting a curse.

Hot anger bubbling, Mercy continued suturing. She heard the door open and Ellen's voice.

Pastor Willis hurried over and helped the man up, but guided him away from Mercy. "Who are you, sir?"

"I am Dr. Gideon Drinkwater. I practice medicine in Boise. The sheriff got a telegraph about the mine cave-in and I came to treat the injured. What do you mean by letting a woman perform surgery?"

"Dr. Gabriel is a qualified physician—"

"She's lying," the man objected. "There is no such thing as a qualified female doctor. No medical college admits them."

"I've seen her diploma from the Female College of Medicine in Pennsylvania. She helped end our recent cholera epidemic. And by the way," Pastor Willis added in a stern tone, "we telegraphed Boise for help with the cholera, but no doctor came that time."

Mercy had forgotten that. She wondered what excuse this doctor would use for not coming to help then.

"There is no cure for cholera," the doctor grumbled. "I thought my efforts would be wasted here."

"Well, thanks be to God, our Dr. Gabriel didn't take that attitude," Pastor Willis said. "We only lost some seventy souls when we might have lost nearly half our population."

"That is neither here nor there," Dr. Drinkwater said, sounding cross. "You can't let a woman practice medicine here. I won't stand for it."

Mercy tried to ignore her irritation, tried to block out the man's blustering words. Her hands needed to remain steady.

"Why do you have to stand for anything?" Ellen's

clear voice rang out. "Dr. Mercy is taking care of things. You're not needed here."

Not needed? Mercy realized that she must intervene. She steadied herself, dampening her buzzing exasperation with the man. "Thank thee for thy support, Ellen, but this is only the first wave of survivors. We don't know how many patients will be needing medical help. Dr. Drinkwater, why doesn't thee observe me and see if I am equal to the task?"

"I will do nothing of the sort," he snapped. "I will not lower myself to work alongside a female who is posing as a physician. Either this woman goes, or I go."

"Well, go then," Ellen said. "We know what Dr. Mercy can do. We don't know how good a doctor you are."

Dr. Drinkwater sputtered and marched out.

Troubled, Mercy concentrated on doing the rest of the operation without being distracted. She sent a prayer for wisdom heavenward and went on with her intricate work.

Having two doctors would certainly increase the injured miners' chances for survival. If she stood down and let this doctor have his way, they'd be down to one doctor again. Both of them were needed. Would prejudice against her cost lives?

When Mercy had finished the surgery and washed up, she walked outside. Weariness had invaded her very flesh. Her back ached; her feet were wooden from standing so long while operating. And now she must contend with the same old hostility. How could she convince this doctor that they needed to work together?

After the storm, the air was cool and clear, the wind gentle. Nearby, under an oak tree whose leaves were turning bronze, the doctor and the pastor were sitting on chairs, talking. Now she saw that the doctor must be in his later middle years with a pronounced paunch, the Boise doctor had salt-and-pepper hair and an ill-natured expression. Mercy prayed silently as she approached the two. "Now I am free to talk."

Both men stood until she sank down on a third chair. Then Dr. Drinkwater snapped, "Did the poor man survive your butchery then?"

Mercy looked him in the eye. "I assisted in thousands of amputations while nursing during the war."

"I'll probably have to fix what you have botched."

Mercy merely stared at the man. Indeed, she was too tired to argue. Crows cawed in the distance. The sound mimicked the doctor's tone and voice. Ellen joined the threesome.

Finally, taking a deep breath, Mercy looked once again into the doctor's hostile gaze. "Gideon Drinkwater, I am a free woman and a qualified physician."

Drinkwater cut in, speaking to Pastor Willis. "I won't practice medicine here if—"

"Neither of us knows how many injured there may be," Mercy interrupted. "If thee goes, I will continue trying to save as many lives as I can. But I believe that there will be more injured than *one* doctor can successfully treat alone. Will thee let men die because thee disapproves of me?"

"Let's have no more time-wasting discussion," Ellen said, attempting to soothe tempers. "We need two doctors and we now have two hospitals. The church at the other end of town is ready for you, Dr. Drinkwater. You won't even need to see Dr. Gabriel."

"Excellent!" Pastor Willis beamed at her. "Just the solution we need. Thank you, Mrs. Dunfield. I'll walk the doctor to the church." The pastor turned to the obviously aggravated man. "Let's be going then. We don't have time to waste."

Gideon Drinkwater rose and gave Mercy a scathing look. "This is not over, madam." He turned and marched away.

"Good riddance," Ellen whispered when the men were out of hearing distance.

Mercy just sank back farther in her chair. She believed Gideon Drinkwater's threat. He would do what he could to make matters even harder for her than they were. But she wouldn't think about that now. "Ellen, how are things at the mine?"

"They're working their way through the rock that sealed off the original cave-in. They're making good…progress." Ellen's voice broke on the final word.

Mercy gripped the woman's hand. "I am praying that thy good husband will be restored to thee."

Ellen nodded, holding back her tears.

After dark, Lon shuffled as quietly as possible into the dimly lit church hospital where he'd been told Mercy was treating patients. The smell of carbolic acid hung in the air. The work at the mine was done. All around him, people had rejoiced that every miner, living or dead, had been found and brought out. For him, there was no joy and no going back to the saloon tonight to celebrate. The cave-in, the storm and the avalanche had sucked him dry. He should have just gone back to his cot in the saloon and picked up the thread of his normal life there, continuing with his plan to leave Idaho Bend behind.

But, try as he might, he had been unable to stop himself from seeking out Mercy. Before he could speak her name, she was there in front of him. Her flaxen hair glimmered in the low candle and lamplight.

"Thee needs some nourishment and rest." Just as she had the first day they met, when she'd served him coffee, Mercy tended him now. She took him firmly by the arm and led him to the front of the church hospital where the pulpit had been pushed to one side. Tall shadows danced on the walls. She opened the back door and said in a low voice, "Lon Mackey is here. Will thee bring him a bowl of stew and coffee, please?"

He wished she didn't always do that, try to take care of him. "I hear you have competition," Lon said gruffly.

Mercy led him to a chair and pushed him gently into it. "A very opinionated man, unfortunately." She sounded only mildly interested. "I just finished treating my last patient. Soon I will be checking on all here again. Since you have come, it must mean…" She fell silent and touched his arm.

Her words caused him physical pain. He rubbed the back of his neck and forced his lungs to inflate. "About two hours ago, we broke through the final barrier and all the injured…and deceased have been removed from the mine." The memory of the crushed and broken bodies that had been tenderly carried out knotted around his lungs. Tears hovered just below the surface.

I shouldn't have come here—come to her. But he had been unable to stop himself. The desire to be in this woman's consoling presence had been undeniable, uncontainable. He bent his head over his folded hands. She took his hand and held it. He didn't pull away. Couldn't.

Then Mercy cleared her throat. "Thee took the remaining injured to the other church then?"

"The last two living, one of them was Dunfield."

"I'm so glad James Dunfield came out alive," she said, sounding more worried than relieved.

Maybe they should have brought Dunfield here to her, instead of the Boise doctor, but they had been told there was no more room. He couldn't stop the old feelings of loss and failure that the past hours had reignited. He'd done his best but, as always, it wasn't enough. Why hadn't he just stayed at the saloon? Why couldn't he have just been another rescue worker? Why did people turn to him? A bleak silence stretched between them.

The back door opened and he dropped her hand. He recognized the pastor's petite wife and thanked her for the large bowl of stew and mug of coffee she'd brought him. "After this," the woman said in a stern, motherly tone, "you should get some sleep. You look played out."

"I am. Thank you, ma'am."

"They tell me you're a gambler. And that after the avalanche, your quick action saved lives. I think your talents would be better used in a different line of work." With that admonition, she turned and went back outside to the detached kitchen.

Mercy had the nerve to chuckle softly. "She has a point."

Their levity fired his anger. "I told you I like living a free life—"

"Lon Mackey, thee may fool others, though in light of the past day, I doubt it. Thee didn't demand the lead in the rescuing effort, but thee was there. And everyone turned to thee without thee saying a word. Leadership is a quality that some are born with. Thee was born for command."

He couldn't curse in her presence though he sorely

wanted to. "I don't want to lead. I just want to be left alone."

Mercy merely shook her head at him. "Eat thy food and then it will be time to rest."

He began spooning up the venison stew. It tasted better than he'd expected and he resented that. He didn't deserve good stew and comfort. Men had died.

At least the Quaker let him eat in silence. He hoped she would fall asleep where she sat and then he could just slip away. *Why did I come here? She can't do anything for me, for the way I feel.*

"Why aren't you resting?" he asked, unable to hold back the words, letting his ill grace be heard.

Mercy looked up. "I am going to. Indigo fell sound asleep when she sat down over there." Mercy gestured to the shadows near the far wall. "When she wakes, I'll lie down and sleep."

"And if someone's wound reopens, you'll just tell him you need your rest so they should stop bleeding, right?" he growled, scraping up the last of the stew.

She said nothing, making him feel like a scoundrel. Still, he couldn't bring himself to apologize. He'd spoken the truth about this woman. Mercy Gabriel couldn't help herself. She was impelled to help sometimes thankless people. For some reason, that made him angry. He set the empty bowl on the floor and began sipping the strong, hot coffee.

"Lon Mackey, thee has carried a heavy load and not just yesterday and today," she said at last. "I don't blame thee for seeking some ease, some pleasure. When I think of the war, I wonder how I survived it. How any of us survived it."

She passed a hand over her forehead as if she had a headache. "I often wonder if the men who framed our Constitution to continue the practice of slavery would have changed their minds if they had known what it would cost their grandchildren in human suffering."

"I'm not in the mood for a philosophical discussion," he said, hating the disdain in his harsh voice. He drained the last of his coffee and set the cup by the bowl on the floor.

"It is not thy fault that all the miners were not saved, Lon." Mercy's rich, low voice flowed over him. But it didn't soothe him; it raised his hackles.

"Thee did thy best, and some lived who would have died if thee hadn't stepped in to lead."

"I don't care!" He said the words with a force that surprised even him. He jumped to his feet, suddenly enraged.

"Thee does care. That's why thee is so angry."

He had to stop her words, make her stop prying up the scab that covered unhealed wounds.

"Lon, thee is a good—"

He pulled her to him and kissed her. This halted her words, but it also unleashed something within him. She was so very soft, so womanly in his arms.

The sensation was intoxicating. How long had it been since he'd held a woman close and kissed her?

Mercy's gasp of surprise died on Lon Mackey's lips. No man had ever touched her like this. No man had ever kissed her. Sensations she'd never experienced rushed through her, overpowering, uplifting, breathtaking.

Lon pulled her tighter, and she reveled in the contact with his firm chest. The strong arms wrapped around her gave her a sense of sanctuary she'd never known. So this was what the poets wrote of…

Suddenly, Lon thrust her from him and rushed down the center aisle and out the front double doors. Mercy stood, blinking in stunned silence, and then she sank into her chair. The quiet of the church hospital was disturbed by a loud moan. Mercy rose and went to Pierre, who was writhing in his sleep.

She touched her wrist to his forehead. Just a slight fever. She sank to her knees on the hard floor beside him and prayed that he would regain consciousness.

As she prayed, Lon's kiss kept intruding on her thoughts. She remembered everything—the strength of his arms, the stubble on his chin rubbing her face, his lips moving on hers. She tried to block it out, but couldn't.

Why did he kiss me? She had done nothing but try to encourage him to accept who he was. Was that so hard for him to do? Then her conscience pinched her. She was not always up to carrying on her work, either.

After the cholera epidemic, hadn't she spent a gloomy time in the back room of the mining office, trying to hide from who she was? And after the horrible words had been soaped onto Jacob Tarver's window, hadn't she been tempted to withdraw again? *Forgive me, Lord. I'm not invincible, either.*

"Both Lon and I have been called to step out from the crowd," she murmured aloud in the darkened church, "called to carry more responsibility than most." She sighed and rubbed the back of her neck. She slid down to lie on the floor, too exhausted to move.

"It's hard, Father," she whispered, gazing up at the dark ceiling. "How can I help Lon heal and be the man—the leader—you created him to be?"

Mercy woke, the floor hard beneath her. All was quiet. She felt a few moments of disorientation. Where was she? Then she recognized the sound of Indigo's footsteps as she moved through the aisles, checking on her patients.

The memory of Lon's kiss assaulted her senses, bringing her fully awake. She couldn't deny the kiss's effect on her. But had he simply done it to stop her words? She had made him angry with the truth, she was certain of that. But though she knew little of kissing, Lon had not appeared untouched by the kiss, either. Intuitively, she realized he would not have kissed her only to silence her. He never did anything from casual motives.

What if Lon kissed her again? What if he never kissed her again? The second question caused her the more powerful reaction. She realized she wanted Lon to kiss her again. But kissing Lon Mackey didn't mesh with her calling. Hers was a lonely path. Now she truly experienced a loneliness she had never anticipated. She had put her hand to the scalpel and now couldn't turn back. No man, not even Lon, would want a wife who was a doctor. Who could argue with that truth?

Two days later, holding her gray wool shawl tight around her, Mercy stood on the church steps. She watched another funeral procession make its solemn way to the town cemetery. These processions took place every morning and afternoon. The mortician and the town pastors were busy all day and each evening, preparing the dead and comforting the mourning. Mercy's heart went out to the widows and orphans who walked behind the wagon bearing their loved ones. As the flag-draped bier passed, she bowed her head in respect.

When she looked up, she saw two men approaching. Gideon Drinkwater, fire in his eyes, and behind him, Lon. She drew herself up and called upon God for strength and wisdom for the coming battle. "Good day, Gideon Drinkwater." She smiled.

"I have never approved of Quakers," he snapped.

"Letting women think they are the equal of men is a dangerous idea. Now, I've done all I can for the patients sent to me first. I'm going to check on your patients and do what I can for them—"

"I am afraid that I cannot allow thee to do that." She had prepared for this. Usually Quakers did not believe in arguing with others, preferring to turn the other cheek. However, Mercy had decided that to permit this man to treat her patients would be to admit she was not a qualified physician and his equal. More importantly, since she had been told by the relatives of patients that this doctor did not practice sanitary medicine, he could actually do harm to her patients.

"Thee knows that no doctor presumes to encroach on the patients of another."

The man made a scornful sound and tried to push past her.

Lon hurried forward. "Stop that."

Gideon thrust her aside. Mercy lost her footing and fell. She gasped. Lon shouted in disapproval as people rushed forward. Lon jerked the doctor around and put up his fists as if challenging him to a fight. Women helped Mercy to her feet.

"Don't you try anything," Lon threatened.

"Dr. Drinkwater," Mercy said, still breathless from his assault on her, "no man has ever offered me physical violence merely because of my work."

"I'll do more than that!" he raged, shaking free of Lon.

Mercy put out a restraining hand, silently asking Lon for no violence. "I will see that you are run out of the Idaho Territory!" Drinkwater shouted. "Madam, either you stick to midwifing from now on or the next time I come to Idaho Bend, I will see you barred from doing even that. Territorial law does not permit women to hold professions such as physician."

"I believe that thee is making that up." Mercy rubbed her shoulder where it had bumped the door behind her. "In no state is it illegal for women to practice medicine."

But Gideon Drinkwater was already stalking away. "I am going to seek payment for my services and then I will be riding back to Boise. You've not heard the last from me!"

"Good riddance!" one of the men yelled after him.

"Are you all right?" Lon asked her, drawing near.

"I'm…I'm merely shaken." She tried to smile. "Thank thee for helping me."

"I'm sorry you were subjected to such abuse. I was on my way to visit Digger."

"Good. He needs cheering."

Lon nodded his gratitude and headed away. Just before he disappeared inside, he glanced back. His gaze told her much. *Lon, what am I going to do with thee?*

As she turned to walk away, a familiar voice stopped her.

"I just don't like that Boise doctor," Ma Bailey said. "He thinks we're dirt under his feet. If we've decided to let you doctor here, what business is it of his?"

Surprised again by this unexpectedly complex woman, Mercy turned to her. Just the two of them remained.

"And don't worry," Ma said, glancing around, "I won't blab your secret all around."

"What?" Mercy asked.

Flushed with obvious triumph and glee, Ma grinned with cat-in-the-cream-pot satisfaction. "About the gambler kissing you last night." She chuckled. "It's good to see nature taking its course. You and him make a good pair. And he'll give you something more than doctoring to think about." Ma winked, then walked off, chuckling to herself.

Mercy stared after her, appalled. The most notable gossip in town would keep Lon's kiss a *secret?* Mercy wasn't a gambler, but she thought the odds of Ma Bailey keeping that secret were over a hundred to one.

Chapter Nine

Mercy tottered back inside the church, still reeling from Ma Bailey's parting shot. She tried to think of a way to stop the news of Lon kissing her from becoming public knowledge. No idea came to her. It was only a matter of time before the juicy details of her first kiss would pass from gossip to gossip. And it didn't help that at the mere mention of the kiss her lips had tingled and her face flushed with uncomfortable warmth.

Lon sat on a chair beside the pew where Digger lay, speaking in low tones. Should she warn Lon?

The church was nearly empty. All the men who had family had been taken home for nursing care. Later today, Mercy would make her rounds in the community, checking for infection and informing the families about the best ways to help the mine accident victims return to health. Mercy turned her mind to the present challenge—away from Lon.

Indigo was sitting beside Pierre, who had regained consciousness yesterday. But he had said nothing, merely eating and drinking while looking at everyone with the most peculiar expression. Mercy had an idea as to why Pierre wasn't speaking, but she hoped she was wrong. Still, she had to test her theory, no matter how painful it might be for Indigo. The truth always became harder to face the longer one delayed in tackling it. Her sympathy for Indigo weighed on her heart. To avoid Lon, she paused to speak to Pierre and Indigo. Unable to stop herself, she tracked Lon's every word and gesture. Finally, Lon departed.

Unwilling still to confront Pierre's condition, Mercy moved to Digger and touched his heated forehead. "Thy fever is expected," she assured him.

He touched her arm. "I don't know if I can stand this."

She knew he was referring to the loss of his lower leg. She sat down in the chair beside the pew he was lying on. "It is hard." She took his hot, dry hand.

He stared at her, tears leaking from his eyes. "I came through the whole war, and now this."

She wiped his tears with her handkerchief. "Thee is a good man, Digger Hobson. Thee will recover. Thee will still be a good man and a capable mining manager."

"What woman will want me?" he whispered.

Mercy took a small, dark bottle from her nursing apron pocket and poured a dose of medicine into the large spoon lying nearby on a square of white cotton. "A woman who loves thee."

He shook his head, suddenly chuckling. "I know it was a stupid thing to say. I haven't even been thinking of looking for a wife."

Mercy smiled and held the spoon to his lips while he swallowed the medicine. The memory of Lon's kiss fluttered through her. "From what I've observed of life so far, not many men need to go far to find a bride. 'And a man who findeth a wife findeth a good thing,'" she quoted.

Digger inhaled long and deep. "How will I walk?"

"I have already ordered a prosthesis for you. Jacob Tarver made out the order form. Thee can pay him when thy fever has left thee."

"So they'll call me Peg Leg Digger." His attempt at humor failed as his voice broke on the words *peg leg.*

She kept her tone matter-of-fact. This brave man needed calm understanding, not pity. "The new artificial leg will not show in public. Thee will have a slight limp. And remember, thee has much to be thankful for. Thee might have died."

His face flushed from fever and emotion, Digger nodded. "I'll sleep a little now. I'm so tired."

She nodded. "The fever does that. Thy body is fighting for thee. And rest with regular food and drink is the best way thee can help thy body win this war."

He closed his eyes. "You're the doctor."

Mercy sat, clinging to his words—his precious, truly heartwarming words. The route to this moment had been like scaling a cliff, handhold by handhold, while men and women had taunted her. Now she felt as if she'd swallowed the sun. *Yes, I am the doctor here. Thank Thee, Father.*

Silently rejoicing, she rose and checked on several of her other remaining patients. Most were feverish. She had no weapons for fever except for the liquid infusion from the bark of the willow in the dark bottle in her pocket. And no one knew why this worked. The longing for better medicine, better science, twisted through her.

She rose and walked to Pierre—no longer able to put off the inevitable. Indigo was sitting beside him. Mercy looked down at the tanned face that was still handsome in spite of injury. Near the hairline of damp chocolate-brown curls, his head wound had been cleaned. And his arm was in a splint and a sling.

Pierre looked up at her with that odd expression.

"Pierre, can thee hear me?" Mercy asked, wishing she could postpone or deny her hunch.

He nodded, looking uncharacteristically sober.

"Does thee know who I am?" Mercy asked.

Indigo started at these words, her gaze switching back and forth between Pierre and Mercy.

He stared at Mercy for several moments, his face twisted. "No. Why do you talk funny?"

Eyes wide with shock, Indigo looked to Mercy. "What's wrong, Aunt Mercy?"

Her stomach roiling over the unappetizing truth, Mercy went on talking to the injured man. "Thee is Pierre Gauthier. Thee is a miner who was caught in an avalanche. I think thee is suffering what is called amnesia. It can happen after a blow to the head. This young woman is Indigo, my adopted daughter and someone who has been special to you over the past weeks."

Pierre looked at Indigo and then to Mercy. "Who are you?"

"I am Dr. Mercy Gabriel. Thee must not worry. Thy memory will return soon. Just eat and drink as much as thee can and thee will recover thy strength and memory."

"You're sure?" he asked, sounding relieved.

"Yes, indeed thee shall." Mercy hoped what she was saying was true. She had seen a couple of victims of amnesia in the war and they had all recovered in time. But there was no guarantee. Unwilling to face Indigo's crestfallen expression, she walked outside, suddenly needing air.

Back at her office, Mercy was cleaning her medical instruments after making rounds of a few patients with less dramatic ailments—a man with a case of gout in his foot, a little boy with a broken arm, a three-year-old with an earache. Hearing a timid knock, Mercy turned to see Sunny at her door. "Come in!"

Dressed in the same faded blue dress Mercy had seen her in when she was nursing Lon, Sunny walked in and closed the door behind her.

"How may I help thee, Sunny?"

The girl looked at the floor. "I don't need to tell you what's bothering me, do I?"

"Is thee referring to the fact that thee is carrying a child?" Mercy finished putting the examining instruments into a basin of wood alcohol. She turned and walked to her desk. "Why doesn't thee take a seat and we will talk?"

Sunny did so. Mercy waited, letting the quiet build between them.

"I don't want to raise a kid in a saloon." Sunny continued to speak to the floor.

"Is that where thee was raised?"

"Yes." The blunt word was said with a wealth of ill feeling.

"I see." One of the worst things about how women were treated in this world was the fact that there were no good options for someone like Sunny. She had been born into a situation there was little hope of leaving. Society was very unforgiving of women who weren't deemed "decent," even though the same stigma didn't attach itself to the men who used these women. "Does thee have any family?"

"No, my ma died a year ago. A few of her friends came here and I came along." Sunny was slowly shredding a white hankie in her lap.

"Sunny, I will be happy to deliver thy baby when

thy time comes. Does thee want to give up thy child for adoption?"

This question finally brought tears. Mercy took one of Sunny's hands in hers.

Sunny was finally able to speak again. "I don't think anybody would want my baby. And it hurts me to think of giving it away. It hurts to think of it being raised like I was. So lonely. No decent mothers would let me play with their children..." Sunny couldn't speak, her weeping was too strong.

Mercy's heart was breaking for this young woman and for her child. "I have a sister who runs an orphanage near St. Louis. If there is no one else to take thy child, I will write her." Mercy squeezed Sunny's hand. "But, Sunny, I would prefer to help thee leave the saloon and find a better life where thee can keep thy child."

Sunny rose, looking suddenly anxious to go. "I'm a saloon girl. I seen how it was with my ma. But thank you anyway, Doc." Sunny gave her a fleeting smile and then hurried out the door.

Mercy bowed her head and prayed for Sunny, her child and for this world that wouldn't welcome this new life. *God, how can I help her?*

The answer came quickly. Not only did she have Felicity, she also had her loving parents. Mercy pulled out paper and her pen, and began writing.

* * *

For the first time since the mine rescue, Lon walked from the back room into the saloon where the lively evening was in full swing. The mining disaster had interrupted his routine. And he still felt strange, as if someone had taken him apart and then put him back together again wrong. It was like donning a shirt that didn't fit.

But tonight he'd get back to his normal routine. And stay that way. No more interruptions to his easy gambling life.

"Hey!" the nearest man hailed him. "How're you doing? My arms are still aching from moving all that rock."

Lon recognized him as one of the older men who'd helped with the rescue. The mention of the mine disaster made Lon feel as if he was walking barefoot on hot sand. But he managed a smile for the old guy who'd worked himself to exhaustion. "Fine. You're looking in good fettle."

"Come on," the man said, "I'll buy you a drink."

"Later, friend. I need to make a few dollars first." Lon headed toward his chair at his usual table. Three more men hailed him with thanks and praise, so he was forced to shake several hands. Each kind word and smile pained him as if he were biting down on a cactus. Couldn't everyone just let it rest?

Finally, he got to his table and did what he always did while waiting for men to sit down for poker— he made a show of shuffling cards. He let the snap of the cards lull him, mesmerize him. The place wasn't crowded, but conversations hummed at the bar. Laughter punctuated words periodically.

Usually, the friendly sounds of the saloon lightened Lon's mood, made him relax. Now each greeting or comment directed toward him tightened his nerves.

Two men left the bar and walked toward him. *Good.* He smiled. Everything would go back to normal now. He'd spent the past night and day lying on his bunk in the back, staring at the ceiling, wondering why he hadn't left yet. And ignoring the answer.

Sunny had finally come and talked to him, asking if he needed the doctor. That had galvanized him. He'd realized that he had to start gambling again or everyone would think he'd gone strange. And no, he did not want to see Mercy Gabriel.

The two men sat down across from Lon. One was a logger. The other was Slattery with his shock of gray hair.

"We need one more, gentlemen," Lon said, sending the cards back and forth between his hands.

"How about me?" The voice came from behind Lon and the shocked expressions on the faces across from him made Lon swivel around fast.

"Hello," said the pastor, who had ferried injured miners to the churches. He slid into the remaining chair at the poker table.

The cards flew out of Lon's hands and scattered over the tabletop.

The pastor chuckled. "Sorry if I surprised you."

Lon was aware that the saloon was quieting. No doubt not only because of the appearance of this unusual customer, but also because everyone wanted to hear what the tall, thin, blond pastor had come to say to the gambler. Disgruntled, Lon nodded to the pastor and began picking up his cards. "We need a fourth."

The pastor laughed, looking genuinely amused by Lon's suggestion. "I'm Stephen Willis, and I won't take much of your time. My wife suggested that I invite you to the community dinner this coming Sunday."

Of all the things Lon had imagined this man saying, that was not one of them. His scalp tightened with surprise. "What's your angle?"

Willis shook his head. "No angle. Just want to thank you for all you did during our recent—"

"Don't want any thanks." The same anger that had pushed Lon to kiss Mercy into silence flamed inside him.

The pastor nodded, still smiling. "We're going to have a special service of thanksgiving on Sunday."

"What's there to be thankful for?" Lon snapped. "We lost good men."

Willis's face grew solemn. "That is quite true. But all the dead have been buried and properly mourned. And there are many who survived because of the good people of Idaho Bend." The man raised his voice. "The whole town is invited. The churches are going to come together for the service. This service is for the living. To begin the healing of our broken hearts."

The man's final words fired up Lon, boosted him upward. He stood up, knocking over his chair. He dragged in drafts of air, his face flaming. Words jammed and stuck in his throat. The anger washed through him in hot waves.

Willis rose, squeezed Lon's shoulder and then walked out of the saloon.

There was silence in the large room and every eye turned to Lon. The heat drained from him. He reached down, picked up his chair and sat down. "We need one more player." His voice betrayed him by cracking again. Another logger came over, gave Lon a cautious look and sat down.

Lon nodded in greeting and picked up the remaining cards scattered on the table. Then he shuffled and dealt the first hand. The conversations at the bar began again, now buzzing. Lon tried to ignore the sound, knowing all the talk was probably about the preacher singling him out and about his curious and intense reaction to the man's invitation. What had gotten into him? Why had this simple invitation wound him up so fast and so hot?

And why was it that the only person he wanted to talk to about it was Mercy? But after his kissing her like that, how could he just go and talk to her?

Maybe the kiss had set up a barrier between them. That would be for the best. Dr. Mercy Gabriel had proven to be dangerous to his peace of mind.

In the evening of the tenth day after the avalanche, Mercy watched the pastor and another man carry Digger Hobson to the wagon. Pierre walked beside them, and they helped him to sit beside Digger. She and Ellen had agreed that Digger and Pierre would be moved to the Dunfield house where Jim had already returned for care. Mercy still visited the other recovering patients daily and would until they were well enough to care for themselves. She tried to keep her mind on the present, but she could not stop thinking of how Lon Mackey had once again vanished from her life. Could it be because of the astoundingly perplexing kiss? Was he full of regret? Or was it something about her?

Mercy and Indigo walked beside the wagon as it bumped its way toward the far end of town.

"You're sure that Pierre will get his memory back?" Indigo asked, looking down.

Mercy sighed, trying to hide her own worries about this. If Pierre didn't, how would this affect her dear daughter? "I've seen other cases and those men did regain their memories. And if he fell in love with thee once, can't he do so a second time?"

"It's hard to look into his eyes and know he doesn't remember what he said to me," Indigo confessed, her voice faltering.

Mercy took her daughter's arm and pulled her closer. As they walked, Mercy put herself in Indigo's place. Or tried to. Her unruly mind insisted on bringing up Lon's kiss. She fought to keep her fingers from tracing the path of his lips on hers. Did she want her fingertips to feel the kiss again or erase it?

She sighed, feeling lonely even here with friends and her daughter. How could the absence of one person make a sunny day chilly and dismal? *I do know how you feel, Indigo. Lon Mackey appears not to want to remember me. And I miss him so. I've never missed anyone as much. I know I shouldn't, but I do.*

The wagon pulled up in front of the cabin. The men helped Pierre down from the wagon and Indigo walked with him into the house. The men followed, carrying Digger on a stretcher. Mercy entered and took off her bonnet.

Ellen turned a worried face toward her. "I didn't want that other doctor to treat my Jim," Ellen said, wringing her hands. "I don't think he'd be doing so poorly if you'd doctored him."

Mercy went to Ellen and put an arm around her. She heartily agreed with every word, but it wouldn't help Ellen's state of mind for her to say so. "Dr. Drinkwater is definitely not a…conciliatory man, but he is a qualified doctor."

"But he didn't wash his hands or instruments when he treated Jim. And it was plain to everyone that the men you treated got better faster. A few of the other wives noticed that after that quack left, you knew what to do to help their men get better faster."

Mercy nearly smiled at the way her brief, simple teachings on sanitary methods had begun to sink in and take hold. She pulled Ellen into a one-armed hug. "I couldn't have treated all the patients. There were too many."

Ellen chuckled ruefully. "Yes, and you're not the kind to speak against anyone. But I saw you kick that man in the shins and knock him off his feet."

Flushing warm around her collar, Mercy shook her head. "I—"

"You don't need to explain that to me. I felt like kicking him myself."

Mercy couldn't stop herself from laughing. Dr. Drinkwater didn't know how lucky he'd been, evidently. "I'm going to examine your husband's wound and see if it needs another fomenting."

Ellen stopped her with a touch on her sleeve. "I've heard talk about you and the gambler."

Mercy gasped.

"People always have to have something to gab about. I just…forewarned is forearmed, my mom used to say."

Mercy managed to nod. *I must put everything but my patients out of my mind. And gossip never lasts.* But Lon Mackey persistently refused to budge from her thoughts.

In the saloon, Lon sat in his accustomed chair, shuffling the cards, listening to the chatter and hubbub. He used to enjoy all the voices and laughter and bright lights. Now it just irritated him.

"I'll take another card," one of the players said.

As Lon dealt to him, a sudden hush fell over the saloon. Lon looked up to see the pastor again. Lon felt like growling. He reined in his instant antagonism and looked at the man coolly. "I don't have a place for you in this game, preacher. You'll have to wait."

The man laughed. "I came this time not only to invite you to the thanksgiving service and potluck but to remind everyone who worked in the rescue that you're welcome. We just want to make sure that those who helped are given recognition."

I don't want any recognition. I want to be left alone. Lon held tight to his flaring temper. "I'll keep that in mind. Now if you don't mind, I need to win this hand."

"I'll bid you good evening, then." With a wave, the pastor strolled out the swinging doors.

"That preacher's got guts," Slattery said. "I wonder what his church board will say about him walking into a saloon."

"If we're lucky, they'll fire him," Lon snapped. "Ante up."

The other three players stared at him, looking shocked.

Lon ignored this and went on dealing. He lost this game and the next. As he dealt the third hand, another hush came over the saloon. Lon recognized the sound of Mercy Gabriel's purposeful footsteps.

"Lon Mackey," Mercy said, "may I speak with thee? I have a message."

He wanted to slam his fist straight through the tabletop. He even felt the blow as if he'd actually done it. Yet he rose politely. "Dr. Gabriel, at the present I'm working—"

The other three players all rose and tipped their hats at Mercy. "That's all right, Mackey," one said. "We'll just lay our hands facedown, and when you've finished talking to the lady doctor, we can continue the game."

Mercy smiled.

And Lon was left with no recourse but to speak to her. "Dr. Gabriel, let's go outside." He motioned toward the door. She preceded him, nodding and greeting men who rose to say hello.

Outside in the chilly autumn night, he faced her.

"I'm sorry to bother thee when thee is working, but Digger Hobson is fretful with fever and he has sent me to bring thee to him. I don't think he will be able to rest till he has spoken with thee tonight. And he needs his sleep." She gazed up at him.

The light from the saloon glistened in her blue eyes. His gaze drifted down to her pale pink lips and he couldn't help but think of how they'd felt when he'd kissed her. *Stop.* He inhaled. "Let's go."

She turned and he walked beside her. Neither spoke until the Dunfields' house was in sight. "Digger is making the best of the situation. And I think with

careful nursing he will recover his health. Please try
to speak to him as thee would—"

"I know. I'll speak to him as if you hadn't cut off
his leg," Lon interrupted. No sooner had the words
escaped him than shame consumed him.

Mercy said nothing further, but led him into the
Dunfields' house.

He trailed in behind her. In the small parlor,
Digger, Dunfield and the miner Indigo fancied lay
on rope beds side by side, all flushed with fever and
looking weak and miserable, much worse than the
last time he'd seen them. He wanted to turn and high-
tail it back to the saloon. But he forced himself to see
them, not flashes of past scenes from army hospital
tents in battle after battle.

He cleared his throat. "Digger, you wanted to see
me."

The redhead grinned feebly. "Come here."

Lon shot a nasty glance at Mercy. Had she brought
him here to sit beside the man and watch him die?

"I'll get you a chair," Ellen Dunfield offered.

"Digger is doing well," Mercy said, as if she'd
noticed Lon's reaction. "I think his fever will break
in the next few days. I must thank Ellen for helping
me nurse him, along with her husband."

So Mercy thought Digger was going to be all right.
Lon felt the tightness in his gut loosen. He sank into
the chair. The three women drifted away, giving the
men some privacy.

"Gambler, I need you to take over for me at the mine," Digger said, his voice reed-thin.

"What do you need me for?" Lon asked, feeling resentful at being brought here to be asked to do something he couldn't do. "I'm not a miner."

"You're a man who can get things done. I'm getting better, so I'm able to think what should be done at the mine. But I'm not able to do it and see that it's done right."

Lon geared up for a good argument. "I might be able to tell your crew what you want done, but I wouldn't know if it was done right."

"Not a problem. I got a guy working for me who's about a hundred years old." Digger chuckled, sounding like a creaky gate. "He can tell you if they've done it right, but he hasn't got the energy to give orders. You met him when you were running the rescue brigade."

Lon wanted to continue arguing, but didn't want to upset Digger. Keeping calm was important for someone who was running a fever—even he knew that. "I still don't know why you want *me* to run the mine while you're laid low. There must be someone else—"

"The miners will do their best for you because they know you care about them," Digger interrupted. "They won't talk back to you or try to get away with anything. You've already won their respect."

"That's right," Jim Dunfield spoke up. "We all

know that more of us—if not all of us—would have died without you moving things along like you did."

Lon pressed his lips together to hold back an angry response. Why did everyone act as if he'd done something great? "I just did what anybody would have done."

"There were a lot of people in this town who ducked out when the going got tough," Digger said. "You stayed and did what had to be done. So no more arguing. I need to know in the morning."

Digger's final sentence ended the conversation. Lon rose and shook the three men's hands, then turned toward the door. Now if only Mercy would let him leave without having to add her bit.

He nodded at the women who had gathered around the table pushed against the wall. They waved at him and wished him goodnight. He walked out the door into the faint moonlight and found he was not looking forward to going back to the gaming table.

He also found he was more than a little disappointed that Mercy hadn't followed him out as he'd expected her to.

"Hey," someone with a rough voice said. Lon felt a nudge in his ribs. "Hey, gambler."

Lon opened one eye, ready to commit murder. "What?" he snapped.

"I'm Athol Dyson. I come to take you to breakfast so I can explain what's got to be done at the mine today."

Still with only one eye open, Lon stared at the gray-whiskered old-timer who was bending over him. He recognized him as one of the older men who'd worked at the mine cave-in and who'd tried to buy him a drink not long ago.

"Come on," Athol chided, the wrinkles on his face moving with each word. "Digger told me to come and fetch you. We got to get to the mine before the miners arrive."

Waves of disbelief rippled through Lon. "I told Digger I'd think about it and get back to him."

"Well, to me and Digger that's a yes. If you didn't want to do it, you'd have just come out and said so. Wouldn't you?"

Lon asked himself, was this true? Then a thought occurred to him. If he went to breakfast and to the mine, Mercy would be relieved. He'd seen her concern for Digger, her patient, last night. And Digger deserved any help Lon could give him. Another advantage—he wouldn't have to spend tonight trying to act the charming gambler. He sat up. "Give me a minute to shave and comb my hair."

"You young fellers—" Athol shook his head, his long beard waving back and forth "—always got to look good for the ladies."

Lon rose, shaved, dressed and rejoined the old-timer at the back door. "Did you mention breakfast?"

Athol chuckled. "That's a good sign. I like a man with an appetite."

The two of them ambled down the alley and onto

Main Street to the café. When Athol entered, he was greeted warmly. Indigo was waiting tables this morning. Athol and Lon sat at a small table and accepted mugs of steaming coffee from her.

Lon tried to ignore the fact that news of his capitulation in this matter would soon be known to Mercy. Why did that bother him? He was glad to do something to help Digger. It bothered him because Mercy was clearly trying to get him away from the saloon, and because the lady doctor was way too knowing. He was a pane of glass to her and he didn't like it. He didn't want her to think he'd changed his mind.

Lon forced himself to listen to what Athol was telling him about the day's mining agenda. *This is just temporary. I'll do this for Digger and after this break, I'll be more than ready to go back to the gambling table.*

On Sunday morning, Lon found himself standing at the back door of the church, idly listening to the large group service. The two pastors in town had combined their congregations and invited the whole town. The pews were filled with women and children, and men leaned against the walls and spilled out onto the steps.

People were subdued and that hit Lon as the right spirit. Lon had planned not to attend, but in the end, so many miners had urged him to come that he'd given in. He'd just stand at the back and slip out before the service was over.

In spite of his best intentions, he found himself looking around for Mercy, but he didn't see her anywhere. Maybe someone had needed her doctoring. Then he heard rustling behind him and quiet murmuring. He turned and blinked, not trusting his eyes. Didn't the woman ever know when to quit?

Mercy was walking down the main aisle, leading the Chinese men and their families toward Pastor Willis. The murmuring increased to an agitated buzz. Lon gritted his teeth. Why did Mercy want to embarrass the Chinese by bringing them here where they wouldn't be welcome? Why couldn't she see that this would discredit her with the people here? His nerves jangled. And against his will, he prepared to do battle for the woman who never left things as they were.

"I'm so glad you were able to persuade our Chinese friends to come today," Pastor Willis said, stepping away from his pulpit. "As you all know," he addressed the gathering at large, "we owe a debt of gratitude to these strangers in our midst. I asked Dr. Gabriel to invite them so that we as a community could thank them for coming to the aid of our miners."

There was utter silence as the congregations digested this. Then Mrs. Dunfield, with her chin high, rose and began to applaud. Her little girl popped up and began clapping, too. One by one, other women rose and then the whole gathering—except for a few sour-faced dissenters—rose. A few men whistled. The sound enveloped Lon and his throat thickened with emotion.

Finally, Pastor Willis raised his hands for quiet. He approached Chen, who had gone into the hole first. "I believe that you were the man who bravely went into the mine after the avalanche."

A sudden memory nudged Lon. Before he considered what he was saying, he blurted out, "Why don't you ask him why they came to help?" All faces turned toward him. He felt the hot flush of embarrassment on his face.

"I Chen Park. We hear loud noise. Rocks falling. We come see rocks over mine. Bad. I say, woman doctor help wife bring baby. We help miners."

Now every face turned to Mercy. She gazed back with her usual honest-eyed serenity. What would her response would be? She stepped forward. "I am grateful, Chen Park," she said, nodding toward the man, "that thee came to help the miners. It reminds us that we are all human and all need each other. I was happy to help deliver thy first son, and I hope he will grow strong and wise."

"Yes," Pastor Willis agreed, "and please stay for the meal."

Voicing his thanks, Chen Park bowed several times toward Willis, Mercy and then toward the congregation. Then the Chinese began to walk back down the aisle. But as they passed, Ellen Dunfield came to the aisle and held out her hand. "Thank you," she said and then continued, sounding a little uncertain, "Chen Park, I'm Mrs. Dunfield."

Chen Park took her hand. "Good day, Mrs.

Dunfield." Though the man had trouble with her name, both of them smiled. Then at each row down the aisle, hands were shaken as they made their way to the open doors.

Inside Lon, disbelief vied with sincere gratitude. He'd seen the Chinese who worked on the railroads and at mining sites hated and degraded by the white settlers, treated worse than animals. How was this event happening? When Chen Park passed him, Lon thrust out his hand. "Thanks again, Chen Park."

When the Chinese families had assembled at the rear and on the steps, Lon looked at Mercy. Awe expanded within him. What a woman. She was a miracle worker. And he was a witness to this one. The admission made him feel how far he himself had missed the mark.

The pastors ended the service with prayers and the gathered congregations answered the benediction with a loud "Amen!" The women hurried outside to where tables had been set up. Soon the tables groaned with pans of roasted venison and elk, bowls of cooked greens, huge bowls of mashed potatoes with puddles of melted butter and, at the end, a crowd of pies, cakes and cookies. Lon hung back by an ancient oak.

He wanted to leave, but found he couldn't make himself turn away. The mixed aromas of the food and the rumble of happy conversation ebbed and flowed over the churchyard and drew him irresistibly, though he'd halted at the edge.

He'd felt a part of this community during the

cholera outbreak and the mine cave-in. But would they welcome the gambler? A deeper, more disturbing thought stirred within him. Did a man who had ordered men to battle and to death deserve a part in this celebration? He half turned to leave.

"Isn't thee hungry?" Mercy asked, coming abreast of him.

Lon startled against the oak. "Where did you go off to? I thought I saw you come out with everyone else." He spoke in a provocative tone and didn't apologize for it. This woman had a way about her that a man had to watch. She wouldn't wrap him around her finger as she had in the past.

Holding a cast-iron skillet with both hands, she smiled at him. "I went in the back entrance to get this pan for Mrs. Willis."

The mention of the church's back entrance instantly dragged his mind again to the kiss he'd stolen from her there on that night not so long ago. His collar became tight.

"Thee must come and sample the dishes or thee will insult the ladies."

He wanted to say no and walk away, but that would call attention to the situation, causing gossip about the lady doctor and him. So he forced a smile. "After you, Dr. Gabriel."

She led him toward the laden tables. He resented every step and the effort the charade cost him. When they were almost to the table, Mercy turned and gave him one of those smiles that he didn't want to admit made him weak in the knees.

He nodded and headed for Digger Hobson, who was sitting on a chair, wrapped in a blanket. As Lon walked away, he made a vow to himself. *I'll be leaving town as soon as Digger is on his feet.*

Chapter Ten

Several days after the thanksgiving service, Mercy sat in her cabin. It had been a long time since she'd had a quiet morning to herself. How long would it last before she'd be called out to a sick child or some other emergency? She sipped the now cool cup of coffee Ellen had brought her with a breakfast tray. Mercy's mind rolled over and over in circles of confusion.

Pierre still didn't recall anything of his life before the mine accident. How was that going to play out? Lon Mackey had kissed her and was now avoiding her. Why did Lon's drawing away hurt her so?

In spite of these worries, Mercy had been able to sleep in her own bed last night, uninterrupted for the whole night—fatigue had simply overcome worry. Since Indigo didn't have to work at the café this morning, she had kept watch over the three patients last night, allowing Mercy the night off. Indigo had returned a short time ago.

Indigo had told Mercy that every morning, Lon Mackey ate breakfast at the café and then left directly for the mine. Would Lon leave his gambling days behind? She scolded herself for thinking about a man who was fighting himself so hard, there clearly wasn't room for anyone else in his life. She would do herself no favors harboring any illusions about Lon Mackey.

Not that she had room in her life for him, either, she reminded herself. She rose and walked to the window, gazing out at the majestic mountains surrounding the valley. The trees blazed with autumn colors—bronze, red, yellow and orange—and stood out against the evergreen trees on the slopes to the towering Rocky Mountains. It was a breathtaking vista and she often wondered how she had been allowed to settle here amidst this grandeur.

She stopped the rim of her cup at her lips. Curiosity halted her.

A man she didn't recognize was limping with a crutch under his arm straight for the Dunfields' house. His expression was intent.

Mercy turned and placed the cup on the tray where the remains of her breakfast had cooled. She scooped her hair into a tail, twisted it up and secured it at the nape of her neck with several bent hairpins. She donned her bonnet, picked up the tray and opened the door quietly so she wouldn't disturb Indigo.

Who was this man and what did he want? And why did she expect bad news?

Mercy tapped on the door and entered as Ellen called, "Come in!"

Dressed in a mix of buckskin and plaid flannel, the stranger was standing by the cot where Pierre sat. The man swung around on his crutch to face her, his expression cautious. "You're the woman *docteur, n'est-ce pas?*"

Refusing to give in to her concern, Mercy handed the tray to Ellen and offered her hand to the man. "I am Dr. Gabriel. And thee is…?"

He squinted at her and then replied, "I am Jacques Lévesque, *Docteur.* This is my *bon ami,* Pierre Gauthier. When I returned to town, I heard he couldn't remember, and now I see for myself. He doesn't recognize me—we who have known each other since we were children."

Mercy looked to Pierre, who appeared puzzled. He should have started to regain his memory by now. Weeks had passed since his injury.

The door opened and a disheveled Indigo entered. "I woke and you were gone, Aunt Mercy." At the sight of the stranger, she halted.

"You are Indigo?" Jacques asked. "Before the mine accident, Pierre and I worked together. He pointed you out to me. I am a friend of Pierre and of his family who lives north of here."

Mercy stood very still, her clasped hands tight.

Indigo moved forward and greeted Jacques. He shook her hand, but kept looking at Pierre. "How can I help my friend, *Docteur?*"

Mercy was torn between concern for Indigo, her daughter, and concern for Pierre, her patient. She decided she must voice an idea she'd been considering, but had thought impossible. "You say you know Pierre's family? Do you know where they are?"

"*Oui, oui,* I had heard that *mon ami* had been injured and had trouble with his memory, but I thought he would be well enough now. I am planning on leaving for home this morning and hoped that Pierre would come with me and finish healing there." Jacques looked pained. "A few supply wagons are headed north. We can hitch a ride with the wagoners."

Mercy took a deep breath. "I think, Mr. Lévesque, that thee should take Pierre home with thee."

This forced a sound of wordless denial from Indigo.

Mercy moved to her daughter, her heart wrung with pity. "Indigo, seeing his family may jog Pierre's memory. He should be starting to recall things by now."

Indigo visibly struggled with tears and then nodded. "If it's for his best."

"It is." Mercy put an arm around Indigo's shoulders, trying to lend her daughter strength. "Jacques, Pierre can walk well enough and his fever broke yesterday. Take him home to his mother and we will pray that she will help restore his memory."

Pierre rose from the bed and donned the hat and jacket that Ellen handed him. He thanked Ellen for

her kindness and then paused beside Indigo. "I...
You..." His expression tugged at Mercy's heart as
she ached for Indigo. "Take care, Indigo." He touched
her cheek and then the two men departed.

Indigo remained silent until the door closed behind
the two. Then, weeping, she bent her head to Mercy's
shoulder. "I love him so."

Mercy stroked Indigo's back and murmured comforting sounds. Regret lodged in her throat, making
further speech impossible. This falling in love was
chancy at best. It came without warning and left one
without recourse.

For a moment, she lost track of whether she was
thinking of Indigo, or of herself.

A week later, Mercy stood at the front of the
church. The ladies who had come to her first lesson
on sanitary practices had returned—and brought
friends for today's lesson.

While she waited to begin her talk, she recalled
the nights and days she'd spent in this building, treating the injured from the mine cave-in and avalanche.
Digger was resting at the mining office while Lon ran
the day-to-day operations of the mine with Athol.

Since Pierre's departure, Indigo walked around
in a daze of misery for which there was no cure.
Would Pierre return and know Indigo again as he
had before? Mercy ached for her child, but dwelling
on what one couldn't change helped no one. She tried
to keep Indigo as busy as possible.

Standing straighter, Mercy began the topic for the day. "Ladies," she announced, the quiet murmuring fading, "today I want to let thee know of something thee might not have heard of but which has been done for nearly seventy years now in Europe. It is called a vaccination, and it will protect thee and thy children from smallpox."

"What's a vaccination?" Ma Bailey asked, from the front row, back to her old pugnacious self.

Mercy couldn't help but grin. "Very simply, a vaccination is dosing thyself with a very mild form of a disease so that if or when thy body comes in contact with a virulent form of the same disease, thy body can fight it off."

"Is that possible?" Ellen asked, sounding hesitant.

"No, it isn't!" a voice boomed as the doors at the back of the church burst open.

Mercy looked up, nearly groaning aloud with dismay. Dr. Drinkwater was bustling up the aisle toward her with a stern-looking man in his wake. She forced a smile. "Dr. Drinkwater, I see thee has come for another visit."

He gave her a scathing glare and then rudely positioned himself right in front of her, facing her audience. He said, "You women shouldn't be listening to this quack female. She's filling your heads full of nonsense—"

"Why're you so rude?" Ma Bailey demanded, leaping to her feet. "You walk in here and treat Dr.

Mercy like a…like a slave or something. You're no gentleman."

Mercy stood straighter, stunned as much by Ma Bailey's defense of her as by the man's extreme nerve and bad manners.

The other women surged to their feet, and a clamor billowed through the church. The Boise doctor shouted to make himself heard and was ignored. The other man, who wore a large brass star on his chest, stayed to the side, silent but with an uneasy expression.

Cringing at the noisy argument, Mercy stepped around to Dr. Drinkwater's side and raised her hands. "Ladies, please."

The women, most red-faced and glaring, sat back down and pointedly gave their attention to Mercy. Mercy turned to Dr. Drinkwater, who looked as if he were about to have an apoplectic fit.

"Doctor, perhaps it would be best if I proceed, and then we can discuss the merits of vaccinating against smallpox later."

"We'd like to hear how to protect our children from smallpox," Mrs. Willis said.

"No!" Dr. Drinkwater objected.

The women jumped to their feet again, scolding the doctor.

Mercy closed her eyes, praying for inspiration. She opened them. She would give this man one more chance to prove he wasn't as foolish as his behavior branded him. "Dr. Drinkwater—" she began. The women fell silent again. "—why doesn't thee have a seat and listen to what I have to say, and if thee wants to give thy—"

"I will do no such thing," he snapped. "I told you I'd come back and stop you. I've brought the territorial sheriff with me—"

The rest of his words were drowned out by the general outcry. Fuming, Mercy pressed her lips together. This man was one of those unreasonable people her mother had always warned her about. "You can't persuade an unreasonable person with reason," she'd said. "Go to the real issue and stick to it." Mercy raised a hand.

Instant silence.

She smiled, knowing that this would goad Dr. Drinkwater to reveal more of his foolhardiness. "Doctor, I am a qualified physician and will continue to practice medicine. Thee does not intimidate me."

He leaned toward her, his face contorted with anger. "Does the sheriff intimidate you?"

Mercy looked to the other man, who had kept his distance and now appeared unhappy. Mercy decided to follow her mother's advice and be done with this irritating man. "Did thee bring the sheriff to arrest me?"

The sheriff chewed the ends of his mustache.

Silence. Every eye was on the sheriff. Mercy decided to push one step further. She walked directly in front of the sheriff with her hands outstretched, wrists together, as if ready for manacles. Was this sheriff as determined as the doctor to make himself a public spectacle of folly?

"If I am doing something against the laws of the Idaho Territory," Mercy stated calmly, "arrest me."

The story of Mercy's near arrest blazed through town within an hour. Lon was seething when he finally tracked down the obnoxious doctor and the territorial sheriff with the big brass star on his chest. The two of them were sitting at a table in the café, eating supper. "You!" Lon declared, advancing on them. "Foolish doctor! I should have blacked your eye the day you pushed Dr. Gabriel down. For two cents, I'd do it now."

The sheriff looked up, his fork poised in midair.

Len switched his attention to him. "What do you mean coming to town and threatening to arrest our doctor?" Lon stood, glaring down at the man.

The sheriff merely gawked at Lon, but the doctor was fired up. "We didn't arrest that blamed woman, though she should be put away where she can't be a danger to others with her quackery!"

"You be quiet, you old goat," piped up Ma Bailey, who'd been chatting with the café owner at the counter.

The doctor reared up from his chair. "Don't badger me, woman. The females in this town obviously don't know their place."

Lon gave the man a disapproving look. Regardless

of Ma Bailey's foolish tongue, Lon didn't want the confrontation to descend into a public free-for-all. And while he was at it, he had another complaint to air. "You're the sheriff, right? What have you done to track down the man who stabbed me months ago?"

The sheriff put down his fork and rose. "You the gambler who got stabbed here?"

"No one else that I know of here has been stabbed," Lon said in a mocking tone. "Have you arrested the man responsible?"

"Well, it's a big territory—"

"If it's so big, what're you doing here?" Ma Bailey interjected, looking as if she were enjoying herself. "Is our woman doctor that big a problem?"

For once, Lon was forced to agree with the quarrelsome woman.

The sheriff frowned and looked at Lon, ignoring Ma. "I came to town to talk to you. I've got my deputies looking for him. And when we find him, we'll arrest him and you can identify him and testify against him."

Lon didn't believe for a minute that the sheriff had come to town to see him. He settled his hands on his hips, still glaring at the man. "I think you two had better go back to Boise. I would think that by now you'd have realized that we've adjusted to having a lady doctor in town. And we don't like interference from outsiders."

"For a gambler," the doctor said in a sneering tone, "you act like you're a pillar of the community—"

"Oh, he's not a gambler anymore," Ma Bailey crowed, rosy with excitement and in her element. "He's managing the mine and kissing the lady doctor. He'll be a respectable husband before you know it!"

A moment of shocked and total silence held them all in place. Then chatter erupted, cascading over and around Lon.

Furious now, Lon stalked out the café door and headed straight for Mercy's cabin. He rapped on the door and walked in before Mercy could even say "Come in."

She looked up from her chair, startled. "Goodness, what is the matter?"

Lon struggled to contain his outrage. *I shouldn't have come here. This is the last place I should be.* "Nothing's wrong. I heard that the territorial sheriff tried to arrest you."

She rose. "I told him to arrest me if I was breaking the law by practicing medicine. Of course I'm not, so the sheriff and the doctor left the church. And I went on with my talk about smallpox vaccinations. Lon, are thee all right?"

He wanted to say, "No, I'm not." Instead, he clapped his aggravation tightly under control. "Why would you tell Ma Bailey we kissed?"

"I didn't, of course. Does thee think I've taken leave of my senses?"

Now he burned with chagrin. Of course Mercy wouldn't have revealed the kiss to anyone, least of all the town's busybody. Why couldn't he think straight when it came to Mercy Gabriel?

His irritation still molten, still flowing, he said, "Fine. Good. Great." He turned toward the door and then said over his shoulder, "Tell Digger I won't be working at the mine tomorrow. I've got to leave Idaho Bend. It's time I finally got out of this town."

With that, he marched out the door.

"Hey!" A hand shook Lon's. "What're you doin' here? You forget to get up for our breakfast meetin'? Digger's drinkin' coffee at the café, waitin' for you."

It was Athol. Lon rolled on his back and stared up at the ceiling. He'd been bunking at the mining office, but last night he'd returned to the saloon. After working all day at the mine and gambling all night, he'd staggered here and collapsed, falling into an almost drugged sleep.

"I heard about you tellin' that sheriff and the Boise doctor off. Still hasn't got a lead on who stabbed you, huh? And that doctor has a nerve stickin' his nose into our town's business. Who does he think he is, tellin' us who we can have doctorin' us?" Athol asked. "My ma always said, 'Keep your nose out of other people's business and it won't get snipped off.'"

Paying scant attention to Athol's rant, Lon thought over last night. He had hated every moment of last night's gambling. Why?

Mercy intruded into his thoughts unwelcomed. He might as well face the truth. He didn't want to spend another night gambling. What he really needed to do was leave the town. But he didn't want to leave Digger and the miners high and dry. At least that was what he told himself.

"Well, ya sick? Or you comin'?" Athol demanded.

"Isn't Digger well enough to go back to work?" Lon hedged.

"Needs his new leg the lady doctor ordered from Tarver."

"Okay, then," Lon capitulated. He rose, shortened his morning routine and was soon walking beside Athol and smoothing back his hair as he donned his hat.

Athol squinted up at him. "Heard you kissed the Quaker."

Lon waited for a rush of irritation at this, but instead found himself amused to be discussing such things with Athol. "You did?"

"Yeah, and you know she's the kind of woman who gets under a man's skin."

This keen observation startled Lon. "What do you mean?"

Shading his eyes, Athol looked to the clear sky directly above. "I'm not too good with words. But here's the thing. Most women're interested in doo-dads and furbelows and such. But the lady doctor's a woman who cares about what a woman ought to

care about—bein' kind and doin' good. That's what
my ma said I should look for in a wife."

"Is that why you're a bachelor, too?" Lon asked,
grinning.

"Ain't a bachelor, I'm a widower."

Lon instantly felt bad for making a joke. But Athol
smiled in reverie. "I been married twice. First wife
was Merrillee and the second was Violet. Both of
'em cared about bein' good to others." Athol slanted
a look up at Lon. "And good to me. If I were younger,
gambler, I'd set my cap for the Quaker."

"I'll take that under advisement, Athol," Lon said
lightly, as if the man's words hadn't been like an acid
wash to the heart.

"You'd be smart to do so," he replied.

Deep in the November twilight, Lon approached
the snug little cabin on the edge of town. He'd spent
a long day at the mine, and it had been a good one
except for his regret over the harsh words he had
tossed at Mercy the day before.

Snowflakes floated down around him. Winter was
coming and this morning on the way to the mine he
had bought himself a wool coat. The change in the
weather mimicked the change in his life. He had
come to town a cheerful gambler, living by his wits.
Now, nothing much was fun.

He walked more slowly, trying not to reach her
door before he could come up with what he wanted

to say to Mercy, how to apologize to her for his hasty, rude words.

The door opened and Mercy stood in the doorway. For a moment, he was transfixed. The candlelight behind her formed a halo around her slender, petite figure. He often forgot how dainty she was in body. Her spirit towered over most other people he'd ever met.

"Good evening, Lon Mackey. Come in from the cold."

Her softly spoken words captured him. He hurried forward and slipped inside past her. She shut the door behind him. The cabin was lit with two candles and warmed by the fire. He was thankful to see that Indigo was not present. "Where's Indigo?" *That wasn't what I wanted to say.*

"She is visiting a friend in town, a girl near her age. I'm very pleased that the girl's parents have welcomed Indigo into their home." She held out her hand for his coat and hung it on a peg by the door.

He added his hat and stood awkwardly in the center of the small, sparsely furnished, one-room cabin. Her neatly made bed sat against the far wall, the table and chairs were by the window, and two rockers flanked the hearth. He felt like an intruder.

"Come sit with me by the fire," she invited, claiming one of the chairs and waving him toward the other. "I thought thee were planning to leave Idaho Bend as soon as possible."

Was she taunting him? He walked, feeling like a

windup toy, and sat down. The chair creaked under him in a friendly way, yet he was unable to relax. "I am leaving," he said with emphasis, "but I came to apologize—"

"For what?" She looked at him, her gaze open and honest, as always.

"I wasn't very polite the last time I arrived at your door." There, he'd admitted it. But he didn't feel any release of tension. He couldn't meet her gaze.

"Thee doesn't need to apologize for being concerned about me."

"That's not what I was referring to."

"Oh?" She tilted her face.

He ground his teeth, then said, "I know you didn't tell Ma Bailey about…" He couldn't bring himself to say the word *kiss*. He fell silent, nettled by her gracious words.

"So Ma Bailey broadcast…" Now she faltered. "What happened that night in the back of the church."

Now her careful wording goaded him into speaking the truth. "You mean when I kissed you."

She didn't reply right away. He waited as she rocked, the chair creaking in a steady rhythm that was making his neck tighten.

"Yes, when thee kissed me." She looked down at her hands folded in her lap.

He had come here with the best of intentions. And here in this soothing setting, with this soft-spoken and gentle woman, every word punctured his peace like sharp teeth. Where was this anger coming from?

"Thee is angry. I'm sorry, but I knew that Ma Bailey would not be able to keep a secret."

"So you knew she'd seen us?" He nearly stood up.

"Yes, she mentioned it to me the day Dr. Drinkwater left. I don't know how she managed to see us. She must have been dozing in one of the back pews and must have heard us…and woke. But as I said before, Lon, I did not discuss what happened with anyone."

"Now everyone knows." His words came out more harshly than he'd intended.

"I have not replied to any plain or veiled questions about it. It will blow over."

Her casual tone and the way she neutralized the kiss—which had shaken him to his core—infuriated him. He leaped to his feet, lifted her from her chair and kissed her again. For a second he felt resistance. Then she melted against him. He tightened his embrace and kissed her as if the world were about to end and this was his last chance to show her how much he cared.

The thought froze him in place.

Chapter Eleven

Mercy felt Lon's sudden stiffening and sensed what might come next. To prevent it, she wrapped her arms around him and hung on tight. As she had anticipated, he tried to pull away. She tightened her hold on him more, refusing to release him.

"Thee did that the last time, Lon. Thee kissed me and then left. This is all very confusing. What's happening?" She gazed at Lon's face. He looked as if he were in pain. Her throat tightened. "What's wrong, Lon?"

He looked upward, avoiding her eyes. "I shouldn't be kissing you. I know that."

"That is not the issue, Lon Mackey. I am not married and thee is not…or are thee married? Is that it?"

"No, I'm not married." He laughed in an unpleasant way. "She had the good sense to marry my best friend."

Realization dawned on Mercy and her heart nearly broke for Lon. "Is that why thee runs off every time thee kisses me—"

"This is only the second time I've kissed thee, I mean you. Don't make a big fuss about it. You said yourself that Ma Bailey's gossipmongering will blow over." His voice was climbing, sounding more and more annoyed.

"I am not making a fuss," she defended herself. "I just want to understand. Thee is an honest man. Face the truth. Thee has kissed me twice, and more than just a gentle brushing of my lips." The physical memory of how he'd kissed her thrummed through her.

"Thee has kissed me with…with ardor. I know a friend's kiss is different than…thy kisses." She took his stubborn chin in one hand and tugged it down so he was looking at her. "Now who is this woman who married thy best friend?"

"I don't want to talk about her."

"I probably don't want to hear about her, but tell me anyway."

He looked startled by her admission, and something changed in his face. "I went to war. My friend paid three hundred dollars bounty for someone else to serve in his place. So she married him. That's all there is to it."

Mercy brought her other hand up and captured his resisting chin within both hands, forcing him to look at her. "What a dreadful woman. Thee is well rid of her, Lon."

"In the end, she did me a favor. She was a woman with no loyalty. You, on the other hand…" Lon suddenly bent to kiss her again.

She stepped from his embrace, though it cost her. She wanted to stay within the circle of his arms. "Lon Mackey, I must be truthful and admit that I enjoy thy kisses, but now we must talk. Kissing means something more than friendship is forming between us."

He couldn't help himself. He grinned. How like Mercy to come out and just tell him she liked his kisses. And how like her to insist on being told why he'd kissed her. He leaned his head back and exhaled. He felt her take his hand and then nudge him back into the chair he'd left.

"We will talk now, Lon Mackey. Thy troubled spirit has long been on my mind." She moved her chair closer to his, but still faced the fire.

A log collapsed in the flames, sending up bright orange sparks. He rose and took the poker, pushing the logs around and adding one from the nearby stack. "Who's been cutting your wood?"

She chuckled. "Lon Mackey, I am not going to be distracted by such a foolish question. Now it is time for truth telling. A faithless woman abandoned thee for a friend. That is hurtful, but I cannot believe that is the reason thee denies who and what thee are."

He nearly snapped, "Who am I then? And what?"

He caught himself. If he asked this woman those rhetorical questions, it was predictable that she would give him her opinions. And she had stated the truth. Janette's betrayal had not given him this deep hurt, this deep ache.

"Thee has no answer for me then?"

He sat back down. Her simple words were aggravating him, and he was aggravated at himself for being annoyed. "Why don't you tell me?"

She began rocking. "I already have told thee and on more than one occasion. This time thee must tell me what I do not know about you."

"I don't want to talk about me," he said, hating the belligerence in his voice.

"Has thee told anyone about what troubles thee? Why thee decided to become a gambler? Is there someone better than I who is willing to listen and understand?"

He pictured her with her stethoscope to his chest, listening to his heart. "Want to diagnose my illness?" he quipped.

She turned and looked at him full in the face. Firelight flickered shadows over her pale features. How had she become so beautiful to him? "I want to understand thee. I want thee to understand thyself so thee stops kissing me and leaving. And I want thee to stop going back to the saloon to gamble when thee knows thee doesn't want to."

He began marshaling his arguments to avoid disclosure. Then he stopped. His feelings had suddenly ignited. Scorching fury surveyed within him. "I'm so angry," he blurted out.

She nodded. "I know. What fires thy wrath?"

The erupting anger became a volcano like ancient Pompeii. It uncapped inside him, scalding and bubbling. He felt her cool hand rest on his forearm. He tried to pull away.

She held tight. "Please, Lon Mackey, here in this room, just the two of us, thee can tell me. Purge the anger. I can stand the storm."

An image flashed in his mind. Mercy and he at the mine, the storm pounding above. Drenched, they were running hand in hand. Another image seared across that one. In the midst of battle, he was urging his men forward. Grapeshot and bullets were whizzing through the air. His men were falling around him. He heard them screaming, calling for God. Fear and terror forced him out of his chair.

"Don't leave me, Lon." Her voice was urgent, yet gentle and completely disarming.

He moaned God's name and then sank back into the chair and began sobbing. He tried to stop the wrenching cries that boiled up from deep inside him. He couldn't. He buried his face in his hands. Mercy knelt in front of him and wrapped herself around him, laying her head on his arm, a sweet presence. Tears poured down his face. Time passed, but he could not stop until finally he was empty, purged.

Finally, he opened his eyes and looked down. Mercy's white-blond hair had come loose and flowed onto his lap. It reminded him of a painting he'd seen once of angels with hair like spun white-gold. *Mercy, what are you doing to me?* "I'm sorry," he said, his voice still thick from weeping.

She raised her head and looked up into his face, a tender smile curving her pale pink lips. "Thee has nothing to apologize for. Thee has been carrying that heavy, sorrowful burden much too long."

"Crying doesn't do any good." He wiped his wet face with his hands.

"Oh, that's right. Boys don't cry." She tilted her head. "But, in truth, they do, and men should sometimes, too. God gave us the ability to weep because sometimes we must weep. Jesus wept at the grave of a friend. Is thee better, stronger than he?" She rose then.

He wanted to pull her back, keep her close. His arms reached for her, and then he remembered that she didn't belong to him. He let them fall back to the chair arms.

She leaned forward and kissed his cheek, a soft, fleeting benediction he wished he could save. Then she sat in her chair and lifted some white yarn from the oak basket on the floor next to her. "Tell me."

"Tell you? What?"

She gave him a narrowed look as if scolding him. "About the war. What thee hated most. Who thee misses most. What keeps coming up in thy mind that has the power to make thee try to be a different man?"

"That's a lot of talking." He snorted. His limbs felt weak as if he'd just been ridden hard and put away wet. He couldn't have stood up if he wanted to. "It's too much."

"I agree," Mercy said. "It was a long, devastating war and the losses to all were overwhelming. Thee knows that I was there, too. Sometimes I wonder how I did what I did."

His head felt heavy. Bending, he leaned his cheek on his upturned hand, hiding his face from her gaze. "I'm spent."

"Weeping takes more energy than one would imagine."

He leaned his head back against the chair and began rocking. The woman near him began knitting, and the rhythm of the needles joined the creaking of the two rockers. It had been a very long time since he felt this much at peace. The weeping had cleansed him somehow. Washed away the sins of the past. *I'm becoming poetical,* he jeered at himself.

Mercy knitted, clicking her wooden needles, and Lon rocked, matching her rhythm with the creaking of the chair. It was a companionable quiet, peaceful. She didn't push him to reveal more, but he knew she would not let this go. "You're right," he admitted at last. "I don't want to gamble anymore. I used to, but that's changed."

"Thee needed a break from responsibility. I see that." She paused, studying her knitting. "But I think that the cholera epidemic and then the mining accident forced thee to face who thee really is."

"And who am I, really?" The fact that she insisted she knew him better than he did remained irksome.

"Thee is Lon Mackey, a good man, a born leader. Thee has a path, too. The war wasn't meant to be thy path—"

"I thought it was when I went to West Point," he interrupted. Uncapped by her fearless words, emotions he couldn't identify easily were sliding, swirling through him. "I wanted to be an officer in the U.S. Army. And we see how wise that was."

I've lost all my youthful zeal and idealism, Mercy. I can't get it back no matter what I do.

He gave a dry laugh. "Colonels are not as needed as before. What would you suggest I choose as a career now?" He couldn't keep the mocking note from his tone, even though it was directed at himself, not her.

"Thee must find that thyself. I have faith, however, that God will show thee the work, the path He has for thee if thee asks Him." Her hands, pale in the dim light, worked the needles and white yarn.

Lon still couldn't wrap his mind around this woman's God. The faith he'd been raised with had failed him in the war. He'd called out to God during the cave-in, but that was not faith, merely desperation. "It's as simple as that?" he asked with an edge to his tone.

"People like to make God complicated. But once

thee accepts that He is God, Ruler of all who live, life becomes easier. He has a plan for each life."

"God didn't hear my prayers in the war. Why would He now?" he grumbled. The old question still hooked him with a barb.

"We live in a fallen world. People like to think that God wants them to go to war in His name, but God doesn't want war any more than you do, Lon Mackey. Thee prayed and thy prayers did not appear to be answered because the war went on and on. But God cannot make humans do something they do not want to do. The Confederacy would not surrender until it could no longer go on."

"So evil exists because people won't surrender to good?" he asked sardonically.

"Yes, thee has stated it very well." She was counting her stitches on one needle, moving them two by two. "If we all put our efforts into doing the good for others that God wants for us, this world would be a better place."

How could he argue with her about that? He didn't have the strength to form more words. But his mind took him back to the war. The few times he'd tried to protect his men in battle, his caution had only caused more loss of life. *I don't have your faith, Mercy. I don't see any path for me.*

"Lon, how long will thee deny they true self and God? Thee does not want to play the gambler any more than thee truly wants to leave this town."

He went to counter her words, but couldn't make the effort.

The door opened and Indigo walked in, letting in a rush of chill wind. "I'm home, Aunt Mercy— Oh!"

Lon rose from the rocker, feeling at least eighty years old. Mercy had exhausted him. "Good evening, Indigo."

"Good evening, sir. I didn't know you were visiting."

"We were just talking," he said, feeling vulnerable, yet certain Mercy wouldn't betray knowledge of his loss of control. How had this happened? He hadn't wept like this even during the war over his fallen comrades in arms.

"If you two want to speak in private, I'll go see Mrs. Dunfield," Indigo offered, staying by the door.

"No, no." He went to the pegs and donned his hat and coat. "I'll see you ladies around town then."

"Please think about what we have discussed. I will be praying that thee finds thy path." Mercy had turned to him, casting her face in shadow. Still, her bright hair gleamed in the low light.

He conquered the urge to return and kiss her good-night. "Indeed I will. Good night." He opened the door and stepped out into the cold night. The darkness around him reflected his dim outlook. What was he going to work at now? And when could he kiss Mercy again? That last was a perilous question. She demanded a lot with her kisses. Would he ever live up to her expectations? Or would he merely disappoint her? Could he live with himself if he did?

In the café's clatter of dishes and silverware and surrounding chatter, Digger, Athol and Lon sat around a table the next morning.

"Lon, I still need you for about a week or two," Digger said. "I can walk now with this prosthetic leg but I don't have the stamina I need to work sunup to sundown. I'll go to the mine in the morning to look matters over, go back to the mining office and come back just before the end of the day."

Lon nodded. He had been expecting this. But the question of what he would do now loomed, mocking him.

"Are you…I don't think…well…" Digger stammered.

"I'm not going back to gambling, if that's what you're trying to ask." Lon felt his mouth twist down on one side. "But I don't know what I can do to make a living. The only thing I know besides gambling is the army." He tossed up both hands and then folded his arms over his chest.

Both men surprised him by looking as if they'd expected his words. "You're an educated man, aren't ya?" Athol asked.

Lon nodded, watching the two closely. They couldn't really be serious.

"Well, then, you ever think of reading the law?"

Digger asked. "Or maybe getting some territorial job?"

"Digger's right," Athol agreed. "You could do somethin' like that easy."

Lon lifted his coffee cup to his lips, playing for time. He lacked the will to take any of these suggestions, couldn't take them seriously. He still felt flattened from last night. When would what the French called *joie de vivre* return? Or would it ever return? "I'm grateful for your confidence in me."

Athol squinted at him and Digger looked as if he were weighing Lon's words.

"Well, you'll have to find your own way," Digger said at last. "But if you need a good word, feel free to give my name."

That struck a chord deep inside Lon. "Thanks," he managed to say. They ended their breakfast meeting and headed off toward the mine for the day.

Hours later, Lon walked back into town alone. His conversation with Mercy the night before and his talk this morning with Digger had finally stirred him to action. He couldn't let them persuade him to venture forth into paths that would bring failure to him and disappointment to them. His mind cleared. He wouldn't delay. As soon as Digger no longer needed him, he would pack up and leave the next day. He walked through the swinging doors of the saloon and was hailed by the bartender.

"Hi, Tom," Lon greeted him and leaned against the bar.

"I hear your job at the mine is almost over," Tom said.

Lon was amazed again how fast news spread through Idaho Bend. Someone must have been listening to his conversation at the café in the morning. "Digger's getting back to work."

"You'll be back again, then?" Tom looked at him sideways as he swabbed the bar with a wet cloth.

Lon grinned. Tom's tone told him the bartender didn't expect him back. "Digger thinks I should change my line of work."

"Well, you know, what we need in town here is a bank." Tom paused and looked at him.

Lon burst out laughing. "You think I've got enough money to start up a bank?"

"No, but you're the kind of man who can go to Boise and maybe Portland and Seattle and get investors interested. It's obvious you're an educated man."

Lon shook his head, restraining the urge to reply sharply. "You have more confidence in me than I have in myself."

"That's for sure," said Sunny, whose shiny red dress could no longer hide her delicate condition. She walked up beside Lon. "Are you really going to marry Dr. Mercy?"

Lon did a quick burn at the town's infernal nosiness. "Dr. Gabriel is a fine lady. Any man would be proud to have her favor. But there's been no talk of marriage."

"Well," Tom said, "she's not the kind of woman you can kiss without it meaning something."

"Thank you for explaining that to me," Lon said, heading into the back room to collect his few possessions. Moments later, he walked out of the saloon with a wave. He couldn't get away soon enough. This town was way too interested in him and the doctor.

His thoughts were interrupted by the sound of firecrackers going off nearby. Along with everyone else on the street, he turned and saw that it was coming from the alley behind Tarver's store. Mercy's office! He began to run, and others who obviously jumped to the same conclusion joined him.

He arrived in front of her office and gaped at the simple one-word message soaped onto the window: LEAVE. A burned string lay before the door, the remnants of the firecrackers. Lon looked around, hoping Mercy was nowhere nearby. "Quick! Let's get this wiped off—"

Carrying her black bag, Mercy appeared in the alley and looked puzzled by the crowd of people clustered around her office door. Everyone parted, letting her pass. She halted at the door and stood very still.

Lon watched her light complexion turn pink and then pale again. He clenched his fists, wanting to batter the culprit to a bloody mass. "I'll get it off," he muttered.

She glanced at him, her face drawn and sad. "If

thee please, I would be grateful." Then she unlocked her door and went inside.

Tarver bustled up with a buckle of water and a couple of rags. "I'll help you wash it off. I wish I knew who was doing this. I'd like to box his ears."

After rolling up his sleeves, Lon accepted the wet rag and began washing the window. His intention to steer clear of the Quaker frustrated yet again. *I intend to find out who's doing this, and when I do, I'll run the rat right out of town. Then I'll go, too.*

Mercy sat in her office for a long time after the unpleasant word had been wiped away. She was fighting the urge to go home to her cabin and hide. Why did such opposition hit her much harder here? She had faced the same anger when she'd entered the nursing profession and worked with Clara Barton. She closed her eyes and pinched the bridge of her nose.

Indigo walked in. "I don't want to cook this evening. Let's go to the café for supper."

Mercy gazed at her daughter. Inside Mercy, unruly emotions clamored, insisting she go home to the cabin, shut the door and not face anyone for days. She forced herself to rise from her office chair. "I think that's a wonderful idea."

Mercy turned down the wick in her oil lamp and blew out the flame. Then she donned her bonnet and wool cape. Outside, she slipped her arm through Indigo's for the short walk to the cheery café.

As soon as they entered, Mercy saw Lon sitting with Digger. This did not help Mercy's mood. Still daunted or distressed somehow by the one-word message on her window, she tried not to glance his way, as if she were embarrassed that he'd had to help her in that way.

Gossip about them was sweeping its way through town as it was. She would do nothing to add any fuel to it. The coffee in her cup rippled from the slight trembling in her hand. She pulled herself together and smiled at Indigo as they sat down.

When the bell on the café door rang, Mercy looked up. Her spirits sank lower than she thought they could. *No, Lord, not him, not now. Help.* Blinking away tears, she murmured to Indigo, "Dr. Drinkwater has just walked in."

"Oh, no," Indigo whispered.

Mercy didn't like the self-satisfied look on the doctor's less-than-attractive face. The sheriff wasn't with him. Instead, a lean man of medium height wearing a small brass star followed him inside. The two of them made their way to Mercy's table. The other diners stopped speaking and the café grew quiet—only the sounds of the cook in the kitchen behind the dining room were audible. Mercy's stomach clenched, but she kept her polite smile in place.

When Dr. Drinkwater reached her table, he stepped aside. The other man stopped beside Indigo, pulled a paper out of his pocket and began reading, "Indigo

Gabriel, I, Martin Blank, do arrest you for breaking the law of the Idaho Territory—"

The rest of his words were drowned out by the exclamations from the other diners. Mercy's mind had halted on the word *arrest*. She closed her eyes and prayed for strength and wisdom. Then, in the midst of the hubbub, Mercy rose, her heart beating fast.

This quieted the café. She forced herself to stay outwardly calm. "Who are thee? Is thee trying to arrest my daughter? On what charge?"

"I'm Territorial Deputy Martin Blank," the man with the star replied. "The 1857 constitution prohibits new in-migration of Negroes, as well as making illegal their ownership of real estate and entering into contracts. They were also denied the right to sue in court. It's all in Article 1, Section 35. Therefore, this warrant for the arrest of Indigo Gabriel was ordered by the Circuit Territorial Judge Chance Solomon." The deputy looked up from the paper.

"May I read that, please?" Mercy held out her hand.

"See what I mean?" Dr. Drinkwater mocked her. "This woman thinks she's the equal of a man."

Though she was tempted to lash out at him, Mercy stared hard into the doctor's face and kept her hand out. She willed herself to hold on, give no quarter. Finally, the deputy handed her the paper. She read it and went colder inside. The warrant said exactly what he'd stated. "Idaho Territory has an exclusion law?"

"Yes." Dr. Drinkwater looked elated. "And if I have anything to say about it, we'll add an amendment excluding quack women doctors."

"Well, if they had a law against quack male doctors, they'd run you out of the territory!" Ma Bailey announced. "You're just jealous because Dr. Mercy's a better doctor than you." Many diners agreed to this loudly.

Dr. Drinkwater's face became mottled with red and white blotches, and for a moment, he couldn't speak.

Mercy handed the paper back to the deputy. "I believe that this exclusion law is against the Constitution of the United States. The Thirteenth Amendment freed the slaves, and the Fourteenth Amendment enfranchised male Negroes. How is it possible to exclude American citizens from any territory?"

"That's not for me to say, ma'am," the deputy replied, rolling the paper scroll-like. "It's just my duty to arrest this woman and take her back to Boise for trial."

At this, the men in the café rose as one. Lon quickly covered the short distance to Mercy's table. "We're not letting you take Indigo out of this town," Lon said.

"Yes," Digger, at Lon's elbow, agreed. "If you have to arrest her, fine. But she's staying here. The circuit judge will see to her case when he comes here next week."

Indigo edged around the table away from the deputy. Heartened by the men's support, Mercy wrapped her arms around her daughter and glared at the two interlopers. Her heart was sending her blood out in strong waves and her face felt flushed. "Dr. Drinkwater, thee is a coward. Thee cannot drive me from the territory, so thee moves against my daughter."

"I told you, woman, I'd see you run out of the territory," he blustered. "And you broke the law bringing this black girl into white territory."

"And I said we're not letting you take this young woman from our town. You can arrest her and put her in Dr. Gabriel's custody." Lon spoke with stern authority in his voice. "Do I make myself clear?"

The men in the room all drew out guns. Shock flashed through Mercy like chilled blood. "Please, I don't want any violence."

"There isn't going to be any," Lon said, with steel in his voice. "We've all witnessed the serving of the arrest warrant. And we'll all make sure this young woman is here when the circuit judge arrives. But Miss Indigo stays in Idaho Bend. We're not letting you take her anywhere. She's an innocent woman and we won't allow it."

"That's right," Digger agreed. And the rest of the men in the café made their agreement loud and clear.

Dr. Drinkwater looked ready to explode. The deputy gazed around, a shocked look on his face.

Finally, he cleared his throat. "Okay, but remember, you'll all be held responsible for this girl being here when the judge arrives." He turned and marched out.

Dr. Drinkwater sputtered words that weren't intelligible, yet Mercy got his meaning, and anger heated her neck and face. "No, this isn't over, Dr. Drinkwater. I won't be bullied like this."

"Yeah," Ma Bailey chimed in, "we aren't impressed with you, Doc. Go back to Boise."

Gideon Drinkwater turned and marched out, slamming the door behind him and nearly dislodging the jingling bell.

Applause broke out, but Mercy sank into her chair. Indigo sat back down, too, looking stunned and wounded.

"Don't let this upset you, ma'am," Digger said. "No judge from Boise is going to tell us what to do."

Mercy tried to smile in response, but her attempt was less than successful. Many in town had accepted her as their doctor. These were the ones she had been able to treat and help. But the one-word message on her window proved that there were some who still wanted her to quit. What should she do about this charge against Indigo? What would be the outcome? Would she be forced to leave Idaho and start all over again somewhere else? Would she be forced to part from Lon, who had just come to the defense of her daughter in a way that had renewed her faith in his goodness?

After they'd eaten the little they could with their spoiled appetites, Mercy and Indigo walked home through the chilling November wind. At home in Pennsylvania, the autumn would still be warmer and golden, but here the wind blew briskly. However, the scene at the café was chilling Mercy more than any wind. Neither of them was speaking. They finally reached their own door and hurried inside.

For the first few moments, Indigo was busy stirring and feeding the glowing fire on the hearth and Mercy hung up their bonnets. Then they sat down, warming their feet by the fire.

"Aunt Mercy, sometimes I just get so tired of it all."

Mercy knew what Indigo was talking about. *I get tired, too, Lord.*

"Why does it always have to be about what color I am? Why can't people just see me?"

Mercy merely reached for Indigo's hand and held it.

"I know you didn't like Pierre, but he saw *me,* not a black girl."

"You're wrong. I liked Pierre. I just hoped he wouldn't break your heart," Mercy said, aching for her child.

"How could he do that?"

Mercy sighed and sank back against her chair.

The warmth from the fire was beginning to thaw her physical cold, but had no power to melt the ice within her. "I guess I'm just especially watchful about you. You're my only child. I want to keep you safe."

Indigo gazed into the fire. "What are we going to do? If the law says I can't be in the Idaho Territory, how can I stay? And if I leave, how will Pierre find me? If he ever remembers me?" Indigo began to weep.

Mercy got up and hugged her daughter. "If we have to go, we will leave word for Pierre as best we can. We have each other, daughter, and I will not give in so easily. I'll telegraph Boise and hire a lawyer. You won't go into court without legal counsel. This law is wrong and we must fight it."

"Why do we always have to fight things like this?" Indigo's tone was plaintive. "Other people don't."

"Other people don't see things the way we do." Mercy straightened, but rested a hand on her daughter's shoulder. "We believe men and women are equal in God's sight and that God loves all tribes and nations equally. Since we refuse to agree to the popular way of thinking, we will always face opposition, here or elsewhere."

Indigo was wiping away her tears with her white handkerchief. "I don't like it."

I don't, either. "Indigo, this world is not our home. We're just passing through." Mercy spoke the words of a spiritual she'd heard slaves sing in the South during the war.

But it's hard, Lord, never fitting in. She thought of leaving Idaho, leaving her friends, leaving Lon Mackey. *He's still fighting You, Lord. Please look after him.*

As Mercy comforted her daughter, she steeled herself for the fight ahead. And for the possibility that she might lose Lon Mackey, just when she was starting to find him.

Chapter Twelve

Another busy day at the mine past, Lon stalked around Tarver's storefront to the rear alley, his anger over Mercy's unjust treatment still simmering. Light from the lamp shone out into the alley. Mercy was indeed in her office. Was she alone? He'd stayed away from her for the past twenty-four hours because he wanted to calm down before he spoke to her. But peace had not come near his reach. He had to talk some sense into her. Then maybe he'd calm down.

The incident with the firecrackers and the soaped message on her office window, plus the scene in the café the night before, played over and over in his mind. He had said and done little of benefit to Mercy and Indigo in either uncomfortable situation.

He must speak to her, reason with her. He must convince her that he had the solution to her problems. Anger had ridden him with its spurs for years now. If he persuaded Mercy, would his lightning-quick temper calm and recede? Would he once again be able to think and act with measured prudence?

Lon approached the door and turned the knob. He stepped inside and felt the warmth from the Franklin stove in the corner of the small office. He had rarely seen Mercy like this in a private moment. She had taken off her bonnet and her soft hair fell around her shoulders. She sat at her desk, writing in her ledger. She looked up. "Lon, is something wrong?"

The fact that her first thought was one not about her own troubles but one concerned for him blasted his self-control to shreds. He reached for her, lifted her from her chair and kissed her. For a moment, she clung to him, but then she tugged free. "Thee is kissing me again, Lon. Why?"

Her hair gleamed, catching the golden lamplight. With one hand, he lifted a handful, letting it fall through his fingers—silken, enticing, irresistible.

"Lon," she scolded, "this is my office. Someone might see us." She stepped back and tried to gather her hair into its usual knot at the nape of her neck, blushing and looking delightfully flustered. How could he not want this woman in his life?

"I've decided that we should marry." He blurted out the unexpected and audacious words in the most blunt, unromantic manner possible. He cursed his clumsiness. *What am I saying?*

She gaped at him, her lips parted in shock.

That sparked his irritation anew. "Don't look so surprised. Do you think I go about kissing women indiscriminately? You are the one woman in this world I trust, the one woman in this world I must care about."

She stumbled down in her chair, facing him. "Lon, thee does not sound very confident of thy feelings for me. Thee 'must' care about me? That does not convince me. What has caused thee to propose marriage to me?"

"Why do you always have to talk everything to death?" He began pacing. Voicing the proposal fired his determination. He would never be free until he and Mercy left this town behind them. "I want to marry you. I know that you'll be faithful and honest."

"I do not talk things to death." She continued fiddling with her hair.

His fingers twitched, urging him to reach again for her hair, to let it flow over his palm. He grimaced at himself. *I must concentrate and convince her.*

"I only speak when there is something I must communicate or learn," Mercy said. "If thee cannot tell me plainly why thee wants to marry me, I cannot marry thee."

He turned his back to her and continued pacing in the space near the door. The small office felt like a box. "I want to go to California." These words shocked him. But his mind was suddenly very clear. "I want to marry you and then the three of us will go to California."

"Why?"

Her incredulous tone jabbed him. He turned to

glare at her. Why didn't she understand what was going on here? "Because you aren't wanted here, that's why. That Boise doctor is not going to stop bothering you till you leave the territory. So let's go. There will be sick people in California who need you, too." How could she argue with that?

She looked directly into his eyes—as she always did. He read the concern for him there and looked away. *This isn't about me, Mercy.*

"Lon, I believe I am wanted here. I have been accepted as a doctor by most of the people in town. Why should I let one foolish word soaped on my window and one nasty, ill-natured man make me turn tail and run?" Her voice strengthened with each word. "I am not a coward. And neither are thee."

He ignored her last sentence. "Of course you're not a coward. But we could be happy in California—"

She gave up trying to control her hair, her hands dropping to her lap. "I suppose," she said, looking up at him and speaking in a wry tone, "thee will spend thy nights gambling and I will practice medicine?"

"Of course not." Her words and sarcasm tightened his forehead. He rubbed it, trying to ward off a headache. "I'll find gainful employment. I'm educated. I could read law there."

"Why can thee not do that here in the Idaho Territory?"

Her cool question drew the headache nearer. "I've had it with this place." He struck his open palm with his other hand. "I was stabbed here. Now this doctor is harassing you. Let's go. Start fresh in California."

She shook her head stubbornly. "I will not run."

He wanted to lift her out of her chair and shake her. "It isn't worth the fight. *Now* some of these townspeople accept you. But wait and see—if a male doctor comes to town, they'll drop you like a hot rock. You can't count on them. The people here will let you down."

"I don't think so," she said slowly.

"You don't know that for sure. And there's worse coming. Have you considered Indigo? Do you want to put her through the indignity of a trial? To make her go through that public humiliation?"

"I hope it won't come to that." She wouldn't meet his eyes.

"What's going to stop it from coming to that— I've just proposed marriage to you. Isn't that of more importance to you than Dr. Drinkwater?"

Mercy gazed at him, mouth open and wordless.

"Do you love me or not?" Lon asked.

"Thee has not spoken of love—"

"I will," he cut her off, enjoying the sensation of at last leaving her without much to say, "if that will persuade you to leave with me. Do you love me?"

Mercy fussed with papers on her desk.

The door opened and Ma Bailey walked in. "Oh!" she exclaimed, looking back and forth between the two of them with palpable curiosity and glee. She must have seen him heading here and followed him.

"What can I do for thee, Ma Bailey?" Mercy asked in a colorless voice, blushing.

"I hope I'm not interrupting anything…private," Ma said, thick innuendo layering her words.

"No, we were discussing this business with Indigo," Mercy responded with aplomb and a lift of her chin.

"That Boise doctor sure has his nerve," the older woman agreed, her face darkening. "Anyway, I just wanted to let you know my daughter and her man arrived in town today."

Lon gritted his teeth to keep from sending the woman away with a few choice, pithy words he'd long wanted to unleash upon her.

"Well, that is good news." Mercy smiled. "I'm sure thee is glad to have her safely here with thee."

"I am." Ma glanced at both of them. Her eyes spoke volumes of nosiness.

Lon paced again, sure that this private tête-à-tête would be broadcast through the community within hours. The headache began throbbing right under one eyebrow.

"I'll leave you two alone then." The older woman left with a wave and a self-satisfied grin.

Lon halted in front of Mercy and leaned toward her. "If for nothing else, come with me and get away from that snooping, meddlesome woman."

Mercy grinned but then grew somber. "No matter

where we would go—" she reached up and touched his hair, smoothing it back from his face, soothing the pounding of his headache "—there would be a Ma Bailey there, too."

He shoved his hands into his pockets and hovered over Mercy, willing her to agree with him. "I want to leave this town. And I want you and Indigo to go with me."

She gazed up at him with maddening calm. "I must not leave till I know that is what God wants me to do. Until then I will stay and fight."

Lon gritted his teeth. When was this woman going to realize that their lives were *their* lives and they must live them their own way? He tried to put this into persuasive words.

He couldn't. He made a sound of disgust and walked out into the brisk evening. Why couldn't she see that she was setting herself and Indigo up for indignity and scorn? Could he bear to stand by and watch?

Mercy woke to a knock on her door. "Who is it?" she called.

"It's me, Sunny. My time's come."

Mercy quickly opened the door. "Come in. How long has thee been having contractions?"

Groaning, Sunny entered and halted, clutching the back of a chair. "For most of the night. I finally decided—" Sunny paused, wincing "—I didn't want to have the baby in my room over the saloon so…I decided to come here."

Mercy reached for her robe on the end of the bed. Indigo sat up and rubbed her eyes. "Indigo, Sunny will need the bed. Will thee prepare it for her?"

Indigo yawned and nodded, rising.

Mercy helped Sunny sit on the chair. Then she turned to hang the full iron kettle on the hook over the fire. She added some more wood to the fire and stirred the coals. Soon Indigo had the bed ready. And then Mercy started walking Sunny. The contractions came closer and closer and stronger and stronger.

Dawn was just breaking at its fullest when Mercy helped Sunny's little girl into the world. The exhausted woman wept and laughed, touching her little one gently.

Watching Sunny hold her newborn daughter brought tears to Mercy's eyes. Every baby was a gift from God. Would she ever hold a newborn of her own? It was a startling idea—one she'd never had before. Lon, of course, or kissing Lon was what had put this in her mind. How would this all turn out in the end? She knew she didn't have the power to change Lon's mind and heart. Only God could heal the pain of the past. Then Mercy noticed tears streaming in Indigo's eyes. Because Pierre had not returned.

Mercy drew in breath, pushing all these concerns aside. She'd received a letter from Felicity saying that she would send someone by train to get the child. But

Mercy hadn't heard from her parents, who lived so much farther east.

She decided she would telegraph them today. She couldn't leave Sunny to bring her child—though unwillingly—into the life Sunny had been born into. Sunny obviously didn't want that. And Mercy was absolutely certain God didn't want that, either.

Later the next day, Mercy stood at the front of the church for her latest venture in teaching public health practices. On the table beside her were the items needed for smallpox vaccinations. The scent of freshly sprayed carbolic acid hung over them. Seven mothers had lined up to receive the vaccinations. Mercy tried to keep her mind on this—not on Sunny, who was recovering in her cabin, not on the troublesome Boise doctor, and absolutely not on Lon Mackey.

Mercy smiled, hoping to reassure the women; each looked back at her very anxiously. "Now, Indigo is going to allow thee to see her smallpox mark so thee will know what to expect after the vaccination. Please go one by one behind the screen—" Mercy pointed to the screen set up behind her "—and Indigo will show thee."

The women took turns. As Mercy watched this procession, Lon Mackey's words ribboned through her mind. His visit to her office had tangled her emotions into a terrible knot. She knew she could do little to alter her feelings for Lon. What a predicament she was in.

Lon had changed so much over the past few months that she had let herself hope that he would at last put the past behind him and find peace with God again. And, yes, that they might have a life together. She admitted this to herself now. Lon was angry, and she knew that it had to do with what he'd gone through in the war. He was angry at himself, and at God.

The four bloody years had been dreadful enough to live through. Why would someone as intelligent as Lon hold on to the horror and grief and regret? Of course, perhaps Lon didn't see it that way. Perhaps he didn't believe he had the right or the power to release the past. How could he expect her to leave with him when his life and his faith were so unresolved?

Finally, all seven mothers had seen the vaccination mark on Indigo's upper left arm. Most of them looked determined. A few looked frightened. Mercy took a deep breath and focused on the task at hand. "Now, if thee is not certain that thee wants to do this, thee doesn't have to."

"This really will protect us from smallpox?" Ellen asked, gazing at the needles and the small brown bottle of vaccine.

"Yes, it will," Mercy said firmly. "But remember that thee may experience redness and swelling at the site of the vaccination. Thee may run a slight fever for a few days. Thee might actually get some of the symptoms of the disease, such as a mild rash. When

I was a child, my parents had all of their daughters vaccinated in Philadelphia. Each of us had a combination of those side effects, except for my sister, Felicity, who had none. But we were fine after a few days."

Her mind kept calling up the image of Lon pacing in her office. Had she made the right decision, not accepting Lon's proposal? The answer came quickly: she couldn't say yes to Lon until he had broken free of the past. Until he'd allowed God to make him whole again, and had acknowledged God once more. If she consented to become one with him before that had taken place, it could stunt his healing and leave him wounded longer still. She felt this unpalatable truth like a stiff rod up her spine.

Mercy cleared her throat. "These vaccinations have been given for the past seventy-some years. And I know that they do work. I myself was exposed to smallpox several times during the war and did not fall ill."

"That's good enough for me." Ellen unbuttoned her starched white cuff and rolled up her left sleeve. "I'm ready."

Mercy smiled and began the process of pricking Ellen's arms and introducing the vaccine solution. Maybe Mercy should seek Lon out later and help him see that she was right, that they had to stay and fight—

The double doors of the church flapped open. Ma Bailey hurried inside, shutting the doors against the stiff November wind. "Sorry I'm late!" she exclaimed, sounding breathless and hurrying down the aisle. "I want to see this." She halted and stared at Mercy and Ellen. "I don't see how sticking a needle over and over into Ellen Dunfield's arm is going to keep her from getting smallpox."

Mercy didn't turn. "I have explained it—"

"Did you know that the gambler just left town on a supply wagon heading for Boise?" Ma gazed at Mercy with avid interest.

Mercy's breath caught in her throat. Despair and shock washed over her in debilitating waves. Nonetheless, her training stood up to the challenge; her hands didn't falter in their work. She went on pricking Ellen's skin and infusing the vaccine.

It was good that her hands knew their work because her mind had whirled away from her, her stomach churning with acid. Lon Mackey had gone to Boise. And without a word of farewell to her. What had she done? And would she ever see him again?

When Lon climbed down from the supply wagon's bench near dark, he was chilled to the marrow and stiff. He needed to buy a warmer hat and some gloves. Still aching from the hard bench, he limped slightly, heading toward the brightly lit saloon. His spirits limped along, too. He'd left Mercy behind. He'd finally decided that the only way to make her see sense was to leave. But how long would it take for her to come to her senses and follow him here? He didn't like to think of her facing Indigo's trial alone, but that might force her to leave Idaho Bend.

Putting this from his mind, he kept walking. He'd warm up in the nearest saloon and see if they had a gambler already. He needed to get started making money again. He walked into a large saloon, saw the stove against the back wall and walked straight to it. He stood with his back to it, letting the fire warm him as he viewed the gathering of men.

He observed that a professional gambler was already plying his trade. When Lon was completely thawed, he tipped his hat to the gambler and headed outside to find the next saloon. Boise was twice as big as Idaho Bend and had more than twice the saloons.

At the third saloon he visited, he sat down in his favorite spot in the middle of the room, but near the back wall with his face toward the door. He took off his heavy wool coat and began to shuffle the cards. He suppressed the feeling that he didn't really want to be here doing this.

When Mercy came to her senses and was forced to leave Idaho, he'd keep his promise and find a more genteel way to make a living. Through the yellow cigar smoke, two well-dressed men and a man who obviously worked with his hands sat down at his table. Lon grinned. He broke the seal on a new deck of cards, shuffled them and asked the first man who'd sat down to cut the deck. Then he dealt the first hand, the cards slipping, whispering expertly through his palms.

Yet something strange was happening. Lon had the oddest sensation, as if he were outside his body watching himself, as if he were acting a part in a play. It was as if he'd split himself in two and only one part was aware of this. He shook off the odd impression. Leaving Mercy behind so she would wake up and realize that he was right must be causing havoc with his mind.

He'd left her a letter, which he'd read and reread so many times he'd memorized it.

Dear Mercy,
When you come to your senses, I will be in Boise waiting for you. I think it's wrong to put Indigo up on public display in a court of law and allow her to be humiliated before the common herd. Come to Boise. We'll marry and the three of us will move to California. I'll give up gambling and pursue some sort of work. And you can start your practice again.

Now he forced himself to think only of the cards and the faces of the players sitting across from him.

In the middle of the third game of the night, Lon heard the swinging doors open and looked up. Lightning flashed, sizzling through him. He almost leaped to his feet. His heart thudded in his chest. But he retained enough sense to make no outward sign that the man now standing in the doorway was the very man who had stabbed him. Lon held this all inside as the game proceeded. How should he handle this? Why wasn't the sheriff around when he was needed?

At the end of another hand, Lon saw his quarry turn to leave. That decided him. He leaped to his feet. "Stop that man!" he shouted. "He's a wanted man!" His shouts stirred up confusion. The men in the saloon looked around, exclaiming, questioning.

Lon shoved his way through the crowd in time to see the small mustachioed man hurrying out the doors. Lon burst through after him, drawing his pistol from his vest pocket. "Halt! Or I'll shoot!"

Chapter Thirteen

Still grieving Lon's desertion, Mercy froze in her tracks on Main Street. Four men had ridden into town—one was the unwelcome doctor and the other three were strangers, but they all wore black suits and tall stovepipe hats, the sign of professional men. The judge perhaps? Another deputy? A lawyer? She could practically feel her stomach sliding down toward her toes.

Digger had said the territorial circuit court judge wasn't due until next week. *I might be jumping to conclusions.* Mercy's beleaguered mind slipped away from Main Street. *Lon, I want you here. Why did you leave me?* The raw ache over Lon's leaving Idaho Bend throbbed throughout her whole being, physical and emotional. Her spirit whispered, *Isn't God sufficient for thee?*

"You think that's the judge?"

Mercy jerked and turned to Ma Bailey who had appeared at her elbow.

"I don't know." The four men tied up their horses and stopped at the door of the new hotel that had opened last week. The doctor was now pointing her out to the other three and sneering.

As Mercy grappled with what this might mean, she didn't relish the prospect of a conversation with this intrusive woman. Yet she smiled politely, if not sincerely. "Is thee enjoying having thy daughter and son-in-law with thee?"

"Yes," Ma said in a sad voice, twisting the apron she wore over her faded brown dress and shawl. "But my son-in-law says he won't have no woman doctor tend his wife when her time comes. I told him you're a good doc, but he forbid it."

Irritation crackled through Mercy. For a moment the urge to snap at the woman nearly overwhelmed her better sense. Then she looked into the older woman's deep brown eyes, now filling with tears.

As always, Ma had said exactly what she meant to say without much consideration of another's feelings. Sometimes that was good and sometimes that was bad. But a person always knew where she stood with Ma.

Now Mercy read in Ma's tear-filled eyes worry for her daughter's safety. This son-in-law's verdict against Mercy was an untimely and unnecessary reminder of how the world at large judged her. It nearly triggered her own tears. She inhaled sharply. "I'm sorry to hear that."

"Maybe he'll change his mind," Ma offered, the lines in her face trembling as she fought against weeping.

Her words echoed in Mercy's mind and shifted her thoughts to Lon. The thought didn't ease the pain of Lon's desertion, but it did put it into perspective. Lon was a man and he'd made a mistake. But if he wanted to turn back, he could change his mind.

"Maybe." Mercy put an arm around Ma's shoulders, offering sympathy. "Maybe he will."

Ma lifted the hem of her apron and wiped her eyes, whispering, "I don't want anything to happen to my girl."

Mercy stood there, comforting this rough woman who had a good heart buried deep inside her crusty exterior and nosy ways. Resting her head heavily on Mercy's shoulder, Ma wept without making a sound.

Mercy thought of her own daughter. Should she follow Lon's advice? Was she wrong to hold Indigo up to public scrutiny, and perhaps ridicule and humiliation? *Should I have gone with him?*

Usually when Mercy asked one of these deep questions, an unmistakable leading—usually a strong feeling—came to her, revealing a clear answer or direction. How often had she heard her mother or father say, when faced with a difficult decision, "Way will open"? That meant that if God wanted them to take action, He would prepare the way, show them the way.

Here and now, Mercy only felt dry and empty— bereft. She wanted to go home and pick up her knitting and never leave her snug cabin again. She gazed up into the slate-gray sky.

No, I can't give in to that gloom again. Lon is still running from himself. I can't. I won't run from this challenge. No more hiding.

"I'm sorry he thinks that way," Ma murmured, pulling away.

Mercy forced a grin. "I am, too, but I will not despair. Thy son-in-law is new in town. We will hope that as he gets to know people he will accept me as a doctor."

"You're always nice to me."

Ma said the words like a little girl. They stung Mercy's conscience like darts. How often when she was near Ma had she spoken kindly but inwardly let annoyance consume her?

"Thee has a good heart, Ma Bailey. Thee showed that when the miners needed help. Thee didn't hesitate to do what thee could for others that night."

Ma tried to smile, then turned away and hurried toward her house.

It was then that Mercy noticed one of the men who had arrived with Dr. Drinkwater walking across the street toward her. Was he the Boise lawyer she had telegraphed?

Lon, I wish thee had not left me. But I must stay

here and fight for Indigo, fight for myself. Ma Bailey's daughter might need my help and I must stay here for her and the others. Lon, thee must break the bondage of the past completely or there is no future for thee or for us. Father, please, I need Thy "way" to open.

Night folded around Lon as he slipped through the moonlit forest higher on the mountain slope. He was still pursuing the man who stabbed him. And to make things even more difficult, he was favoring one ankle. Someone in the crowd outside the saloon had tripped him and he'd fallen, twisting his ankle. He hadn't wasted time finding out if it had been on purpose or not.

The cold December wind shook the dried oak leaves nearby. Though slowed by his injury, Lon had managed to follow the man out of town and far up this slope at a distance. Or had he lost him? Darkness had come much too soon for his liking.

From behind, a blow caught him in the kidneys. Pain. He doubled up, falling to his knees. Another blow struck his right ear. Head ringing, Lon rolled onto his back. He jumped up. The man caught him with an uppercut to the jaw. Lon began throwing punches. The near blackness made it difficult to find his target.

A fist punched him in the jaw again. For a moment, stars of light flashed before his eyes. Then he came fully back to consciousness. He heard the man running off, stirring the branches of the fir trees and the underbrush.

With the back of his hand, Lon wiped the blood from his split lip and continued his pursuit. He threaded his way between trees. The man must have stopped. Lon paused, straining to hear movement. An owl hooted. Something—a bat?—swooped overhead.

Again, Lon was struck from behind. This time the man missed his kidneys. Lon rode the punch. He turned, and with a fist to the jaw, downed the man. Then, bending over him, Lon planted a powerful punch to the side of his attacker's head.

The man lay, gasping in the faint moonlight. Lon pulled the pistol out from his vest. The man cursed him. "Well, go ahead and shoot, Yankee colonel!"

Lon stood stock-still. He couldn't make out the man's face. "What did you call me?"

"I called you what you are, you Yankee colonel. I seen you." The man sounded as if he were fighting tears. "I know you. Your regiment killed practically every man in my company that day at Antietam."

Bloody Antietam. The worst slaughter of all. But Lon couldn't put what the man was saying together. "What has Antietam got to do with your stabbing me in Idaho Bend? You and I played cards together for several nights."

"I didn't know who you was at first," the man said, panting. "You just looked familiar somehow. And then that night I recognized you. Something you said triggered my memory and I seen you again, your sword in the air, leading your men down on us."

"We were at war," Lon said, shaking his head as if he weren't hearing right.

"That don't make it right!" The man cursed him.

Lon stared down at the shadowy shape on the ground. "Are you crazy? The war's over." His words rebounded against him as if an unseen fist had landed a blow to his own head. *The war's over.*

"The war will never be over—not in my mind!" the man retorted. His tone was sick, hateful, venomous.

"Four years of war wasn't enough for you?" Lon asked, feeling disoriented and dazed himself. "You didn't get enough of killing and dying in four years?"

"No. Not while Yankees like you live."

The quick, hot reply shocked Lon. "Why would you want to go on fighting the war?"

"Stop talking. Just shoot me or let me go. I got nothin' more to say to you."

Lon was at a loss. He couldn't release the man he was sure would try to kill him again—and perhaps others. But it was a long way back to town, and Lon had nothing with which to tie the man's hands. Then it came to him.

"Get up," he ordered the man. "You're a prisoner of war. Put your hands on your head and keep them there." Lon waited to see what the man would do.

His prisoner obeyed his orders, just as if they were both in opposing armies and Lon had captured him. Clearly, the war had not ended for this man. It was a startling, stomach-churning realization.

"Go on then," Lon ordered. "We're heading back to the sheriff. You'll be charged there."

The man began walking and Lon followed at a safe distance, his pistol poised to fire. He couldn't trust this man, not if he were still trapped in the war.

A cloud covered the sliver of a moon, hiding his prisoner from him. Would he try to get away? No, the man kept moving forward, his elbows out at that awkward angle. Maybe the man was relieved to have been caught. If he was in custody, he wouldn't be compelled to try to get revenge. What a weight he must carry—trying to right all the wrongs of the war. That was worse than death. He pitied the poor wretch.

Still, Lon recalled the excruciating pain he suffered after being stabbed, and the long feverish days and nights. He couldn't let this man go free to do that to some other former soldier.

Lon kept trying to grapple with what it all meant, how it had all happened. The man's words kept echoing in Lon's head. *The war will never be over—not in my mind.*

Deeper into the cold-night hours and with his pistol in hand, Lon steered the man into the dimly lit sheriff's office. The sheriff looked up from his chair, where he had obviously been dozing. "What's this?"

Lon told the man to halt. "This is the man who stabbed me in Idaho Bend."

The sheriff looked at Lon and then at the man. "You're sure?"

"Yes, I'm sure. Can you arrest him, or do I have to do that, too?" Lon growled, cold and irritated.

Frowning, the sheriff grabbed manacles from a peg on the wall, and with a couple of sharp metallic snaps, secured the man's hands. He motioned for Lon to follow him as he led the man to the cell in the rear of the office. When the prisoner was in the cell, the sheriff slammed the door.

The man glared at the sheriff and Lon. "You a Yankee, too?"

The sheriff gave him an irritated look. "The war's over. If you think you're still fighting it, you're loony."

Lon followed the sheriff out to the office area again. He shook his head, wincing from the pain caused by the blows he'd taken tonight, and then collapsed into the chair by the desk.

"You're sure this is the man who stabbed you?" the lawman asked again.

"Yes, we played cards several times before he decided to stab me." Lon had thought that catching the man would have given him more satisfaction. Instead, he was gripped by an odd feeling. Something had happened to him during the exchange with this

Johnny Reb, the label Yankees had for Confederate soldiers. This Reb who had decided to continue the war single-handedly.

Lon said, "I need a place to stay tonight. Which hotel in town is best?"

The sheriff replied with a few short words and Lon rose.

"Is that it?" the sheriff asked.

"What do you mean?" Lon turned, already heading out the door.

"Well, you sounded all fired up about this man when I talked to you in Idaho Bend. Why aren't you...?" The sheriff gave him a sideways glance. "You don't seem mad or excited or anything."

Lon paused, completely still. He probed his emotions and found no anger, just peace and a deep desire to eat his fill and then fall asleep. "Why should I be? I caught him, and now you've arrested him." Lon shrugged and headed out the door to find his late supper and a bed.

Outside in the bracing night air, he shivered and began walking fast. As if touching a recently healed wound, he probed his heart and mind once more. He found no pain. Instead, there was something he'd longed for but which had eluded him until now. He felt a deep peace inside. And suddenly he wanted nothing more than to get back to Idaho Bend and share that peace with Mercy.

Mercy walked into the saloon, which had been turned into a courtroom. She recalled the night she had operated on Lon's stab wound, and the nights spent in the back room nursing him. The agitating memories rushed through her like a flight of raucous crows.

He's gone. He left me. Mercy kept her back straight and her chin level. She would show neither fear nor pain. Was she doing right by fighting? Or was this court case a sign for her to leave Idaho Bend? *My trust is in Thee, Father.*

Indigo walked beside her with her head down.

Mercy didn't blame her. It was hard to look into faces that held condemnation or censure. The Civil War had outlawed slavery, but what of the bondage of prejudice? How did one fight that invisible war?

The Boise defense lawyer who had come to town yesterday motioned for Indigo to come with him and for Mercy to sit with the other people who'd come to watch the trial. She made an effort to smile at the bystanders she knew and sat down on the edge of a hard chair.

The judge in his black robe, the prosecuting attorney and Dr. Drinkwater entered the room. The people rose and stood until the judge sat down behind a rough-hewn table and motioned for them to be seated.

Mercy followed the exchanges between the two lawyers and the judge. Dr. Drinkwater sat on the opposite side of the room, glaring at her. She smiled at him and refused to show how upset and anxious she was.

For one brief, traitorous moment, Mercy let herself think of leaving Idaho Bend with Indigo and meeting Lon in Boise. *But that isn't what I want. This town is home. That's why I couldn't just leave here. This is where I am meant to be. I feel that, know that now.* This gave her a measure of confidence, but fear lurked, ready to take her captive.

The selection of the jury began. Men were lined up and questioned by the two lawyers and the judge. When she spotted a few of the locals who had openly disapproved of her profession, Mercy's spirits weren't improved. She folded her hands in her lap and continued to pray that God's will would be done here.

In the quiet Boise café, Lon was eating a leisurely late breakfast. He'd slept better than he had in months and had awakened with the appetite of a lumberjack. Now he chewed, savoring the golden toast soaked with melted butter and coated thickly with red huckleberry jam. Delicious.

He breathed in the intoxicating fragrance of bacon, fresh coffee, melted butter and cinnamon. This blessed morning every sight, sound and taste around him was fresh, brilliant, vital—as if he'd spent the past few years looking at life through smudged spectacles. Today he saw clearly that this was a great morning to be alive.

A man with wild white hair sticking out from under his hat came in and stood glancing around.

Then he made a beeline toward Lon. "Hey! You that gambler that caught the man who stabbed him?"

Lon paused, his forkful of egg and sausage halfway to his mouth. He went ahead and took the bite but he nodded in answer to the man's question.

"I'm Jeffries. Own the newspaper here in Boise. Tell me what happened." As the man spoke like he was sending a telegram, he sat down. He drew out a pad of paper and a roughly sharpened pencil and licked the lead.

Lon chewed and swallowed, still comfortably at his ease. "The man stabbed me in Idaho Bend. I saw him here and caught him last night."

"What's his name?"

"Don't know." *Don't care.* "Ask the sheriff."

"Why'd he stab you? Were you cheating?"

"A skilled gambler doesn't have to cheat to win." Lon considered whether he should reveal the man's reason for stabbing him and then decided not to. The Reb had been unbalanced by the war and Lon had suffered something similar until last night.

And did this newspaper man expect Lon to confess to cheating? Though Lon had read this man's paper in the past, in light of this he might have to reconsider what he thought of it. Something niggled at the back of Lon's mind, something he'd read in this man's paper. Or was it in some other newspaper?

Jeffries stared at him, pencil hovering. "I hear you're sweet on the woman posing as a doctor over there."

The intrusion and the word *posing* shattered Lon's peace. "Are you a gossipmonger? And let me tell you, Dr. Mercy Gabriel saved my life and has saved many others this year." Lon glared. "She nursed with Clara Barton during the war and no doubt saved hundreds of lives there also. I've seen her certificate and I've seen her operate. And my only comment is that anyone who would prefer Dr. Drinkwater over Dr. Gabriel is an idiot." Lon felt like punching the man in the nose, just to make sure he'd gotten Lon's point.

Jeffries made a humming sound. "You don't say?"

"I do say." Lon took a long, reviving swallow of the good coffee.

"Drinkwater's been bad-mouthing her all over town." The man's gaze darted from his notes to Lon's face and back again.

"That means he's not only a bad doctor, but also no gentleman."

Jeffries nodded, tapping the pencil on the pad. "I think you're probably right. Now, what about this trial that's going on against the black girl—what's her name?"

Lon froze. He'd awakened this morning feeling so good after last night's capture that worry even about Indigo had drifted from his thoughts. He'd been a fool. "Has the trial started? I thought the judge wasn't expected in Idaho Bend till next week."

"No, he left here yesterday—"

Lon downed the rest of his coffee and handed

the waitress what he owed with a generous tip and a smile. Then he headed straight for the door.

"Hey!" the newspaperman called, following him. "Hey, I'm not done interviewing you!"

Lon ignored the man and hurried down the street toward the livery. He'd have to hire a horse. *I must have been out of my mind to leave Mercy to face that trial alone.*

Chapter Fourteen

Mercy was so proud of Indigo. Throughout the hours spent choosing the jury, her daughter had sat beside the lawyer, straight and composed. And then as the case began, she had faced those who testified about the exclusionary law that said she couldn't live here.

"Your honor," Mercy's tall, reedy lawyer said, "the intent of the exclusionary law is attached historically to the slave state versus free state conflict, which is no longer a reality. The Civil War settled that controversy once and for all. Our Negroes are no longer slaves but free citizens. And as such, free citizens cannot be stopped from entering any U.S. territory."

"Counsel," said the judge, who looked as if his face had been carved from rock, "I understand your case, but this is a circuit court, not the Supreme Court. It is not in my jurisdiction to declare a law unconstitutional."

"A little over a year ago, on January 10, 1867," the defense lawyer continued, "the U.S. Congress passed the Territorial Suffrage Act, which allowed African-Americans in the Western territories to vote. The act immediately enfranchised black male voters in those territories. Doesn't it follow that the U.S. Congress wouldn't have passed this if territories could indeed exclude black citizens?"

"That still doesn't address the coming of new immigrants to Idaho," the judge countered.

The prosecuting attorney—young and very well dressed—gloated with a smile. "Your honor, since the defense counsel has no way to discount the law, I ask that the jury bring in the only logical verdict. Indigo Gabriel is guilty of entering the Idaho Territory unlawfully."

The judge looked to the defense attorney. "Defense counsel, do you have any other witnesses or arguments you wish to present at this time?"

"No, your honor. The defense rests."

Mercy felt each of these solemn, hopeless words like a knife thrust.

The judge turned to the twelve men sitting together along one side of the saloon. "You men have heard the evidence. Now go into the back room, elect a foreman and then talk this all over. When you have your decision, come back out and have your foreman announce it."

The judge banged his gavel and adjourned court. The jury filed out, and the onlookers who were standing against the walls or sitting on chairs began talking in low tones to each other.

Indigo turned around to Mercy. As she looked over Mercy's shoulder, her brave smile transformed to an expression of shock.

Mercy whirled around and saw Lon Mackey walking into the saloon.

She rose. "Lon Mackey."

"Mercy Gabriel." Then she was within the circle of his arms and he was kissing her. She heard the gasps of surprise around them, but she found she didn't care.

"I'm sorry I left. Is this Indigo's lawyer? Is there anything I can do?"

In reply, Mercy remained pressed against him and rested her cheek against his coat. The lawyer turned and shook the hand Lon offered him. "You're a bit late. The jury just went out to deliberate."

Lon's face fell.

Mercy looked up at Lon. "I'm so glad thee came." She couldn't say more, turning her face into Lon's shoulder, hiding her distress.

"I'm sorry I'm late. But—"

Then Mercy looked back up at him, really seeing his condition. "Lon, why does thee have a split lip and a black eye?" The shock of his unexpected arrival had, for a few moments, evidently overwhelmed her normal perception. "Is thee hurt?"

"It's a long story." Lon kept Mercy close.

"We have time," Mercy said and drew him down to sit beside her.

Lon squeezed her hand and whispered, "I'll tell you later."

Mercy accepted Lon's words, overwhelmed again by his sudden return. She reveled in Lon's presence and his firm but gentle grip on her hand.

"This is really a matter that the Supreme Court should take up," the lawyer said to Mercy. "There are black settlers in Oregon State and the Washington and Idaho Territories, in spite of the exclusionary laws. The black pioneers just keep to themselves and are for the most part left alone."

"Well, we explained to you why this has all come about," Indigo said, sounding angry. "I certainly have not done anything to call attention to myself. It's all about hateful prejudice, not the law." She rose. "I'm going to walk outside a bit. I can't sit here." Indigo hurried toward the door and the lawyer put on his hat and left for the café.

Mercy suddenly realized that she had kissed Lon in front of the whole town and was actually holding hands with him. Suddenly embarrassed, she tried to withdraw her hand from his.

He wouldn't let go. "Please, Mercy, forgive me for leaving. I don't know what I was thinking…" He halted. "Yes, I do. I was thinking that—"

He was interrupted by the jury filing back into the courtroom. Their quick return appeared to surprise everyone. There was some commotion as the temporary bailiff, Tom the bartender, went out and summoned Indigo and her lawyer back into the saloon.

Once everyone was in place, the judge returned. Everyone rose; he gaveled court back into session. He then looked to the jury. "Have you come to a verdict?"

Foreman Slattery, with his distinctive gray shock of hair, rose. "Yes, your honor. We find the defendant not guilty."

For a few moments, Mercy distrusted her ears. Did he say "not guilty," or was it just that she wanted him to say those words?

"Would you repeat that?" the judge requested, looking and sounding incredulous.

"Your honor, we find the defendant not guilty," Slattery repeated, looking straight at Dr. Drinkwater. "And we also think that doctors from Boise ought to mind their own business and not mess in ours." The jury murmured their agreement.

Dr. Drinkwater leapt to his feet. "This can't be legal!" The doctor's words shattered the polite reserve of the bystanders. They all began talking, arguing. Their outburst swallowed up the rest of Dr. Drinkwater's rant. Both the doctor and the general public were silenced when the judge began pounding his gavel. "Order in the court! Order, or I'll empty the room!"

An agitated silence settled over the barroom court.

The judge looked to Slattery. "How did you come to this…unexpected verdict?"

"Well, your honor," Slattery said, looking toward Indigo and Mercy, "we decided that you out-of-town people made a mistake. Indigo isn't black. Anyone can see that."

Another jury member popped up. "She's just been out in the sun a lot." He looked at Mercy. "Dr. Gabriel, you need to make sure your girl wears a bonnet and gloves outside from now on. We don't want anyone else getting the wrong idea." He sat down, looking puckishly satisfied.

The rest of the jury nodded their agreement. A few men behind Mercy actually chuckled and a man called out, "That'll teach Boise people to stick their noses into our business!"

The judge pounded his gavel, glaring at the loud-mouth who called out those words. He turned his gaze to Indigo. "Will the defendant please rise?"

Indigo did, facing him, her head high.

Mercy was so proud of the way her beautiful daughter stood, tall and unflinching.

"Miss Indigo Gabriel, you have been found to be not guilty of this charge by a jury of your peers." The judge looked resigned but disgruntled. "Jury, you're dismissed with the thanks of the Idaho Territory." He hit the tabletop with his gavel once more, rose and withdrew into the back room.

The outcome had come so swiftly and with such an unexpected twist that an intense, watchful mood quieted the room. Slattery made his way through the crowd to Mercy. "I want to apologize, ma'am, for the ugly words I wrote on Tarver's store window. When I seen how you took care of the miners, I changed my mind."

Mercy rose and offered the man her hand. "What is thy full name?"

"Irwin Slattery, ma'am."

"Irwin Slattery, thank thee for thy honesty. But I still don't understand how the jury came to this conclusion. Thee all know that my daughter is—"

Slattery cut her off with a conspiratorial grin. "Your girl showed her stuff, taking care of people, too. And besides, we're not letting that quack doctor from Boise push us around. We'll decide who gets to live in Idaho Bend *and* who practices medicine here."

Instantly, a hubbub of voices filled the room as everyone started discussing what Slattery had just revealed.

Slattery turned to leave and then turned back. "I didn't set off the firecrackers and write that word. I think that was kids. Firecrackers is usually boys. Trust me."

Mercy smiled. Her mind whirled with all that had just happened. She turned and saw Lon's incredulous expression, which she guessed must mirror her own. Before she could say another word, he pulled her into his arms again.

* * *

Dr. Drinkwater pushed through the crowd of well-wishers who surrounded Mercy and Indigo. Lon wanted to punch the man and send him sprawling. People let the doctor through, but the looks they were sending his way weren't welcoming. "I am going to take this to the territorial governor—"

"I think it's time you went back to Boise—for your own health. Leave right away so you can get back there before dark. The woods around here are dangerous at night," Lon said.

Silence descended. Prickly. And foreboding.

The Boise doctor stopped speaking and looked around. He found himself surrounded by Digger Hobson and the largest men from Digger's mine. Each one was staring at him intently, unkindly. For once, the man was speechless.

Indigo's defense attorney slid through the men and took the doctor by the elbow. "Why don't you head to Boise with me now? The prosecutor and judge have to stay and finish a few more land cases, but we can leave."

Dr. Drinkwater nodded, his jaw still working as though chewing words he feared to voice. People parted, letting the two men leave the saloon.

The minute they went through the doors, Tom called out, "Well, I'd buy everybody a drink, but court's still in session for the rest of the day!"

Many men laughed and started a jovial argument about Tom's spurious offer. Under cover of this, Lon led Mercy and Indigo from the saloon. Outside, the air was downright cold.

Mercy clung to his arm. "Lon, why did thee come back?"

Lon gazed into her honest, blue eyes and wondered how he could tell her all he wanted her to hear.

"Aunt Mercy, I think you should take Mr. Mackey to our cabin for a cup of tea. I'm invited to my friend's house to celebrate."

Lon grinned with gratitude. *Sharp girl.* "Thanks, Miss Indigo. A cup of tea would be most welcome."

Lon offered Mercy his arm and proudly led her down Main Street. They stopped often to accept congratulations from friends and others whom they knew only on sight. Lon felt as if he had passed from night to day. The fight last night had torn down the high walls he'd built around himself. He could even breathe more easily. And the woman beside him drew him more than ever.

Finally, they arrived at her cabin. He opened the door for her and she led him inside. As if it were his usual chore, he went to the hearth and busied himself stoking the low fire. Mercy filled an iron kettle and hung it over the fire on the hook. Being in her home and doing these mundane tasks beside her touched Lon. It was like coming home at last.

"Come and sit down, Lon, and tell me why thee has a black eye, a split lip and probably other hurts."

Doing as she suggested, he grinned at her in the

low light from the two small windows. "Mercy, I found the man who stabbed me in a saloon in Boise. I chased him down and…" He shook his head, still unable to believe how much had changed within him over the intervening hours.

She put a hand over his on the table. The simple act rocked him to his core. *Mercy, sweet Mercy mine.*

He drew her hand to his mouth and kissed it. "I think I've been changing all along—ever since you arrived in town. But last night I discovered that the man stabbed me not over the card game but because he recognized me as the commander of the Union regiment that decimated his Confederate unit."

He kissed her hand again and was pleased that she didn't try to draw it from his grasp. "He's still fighting the war. And in doing so he's losing his present life. That's what you've been telling me all along. Telling me to let go of the war. To be free of it. Free of the deaths I was powerless to prevent." The final phrase cost him. He had to stop and let the pain flow through him once more and then let it drain away. "I still feel the pain, but I'm no longer angry at God, or myself."

Mercy then did something he would never have expected her to do. She leaned forward and kissed him as if it were the most natural thing for her to do.

"Mercy," he murmured, "I love you." Though he knew he was speaking the truth, his own words spoken aloud surprised him. To make sure she knew he meant it, he repeated, "I love you."

"And I love thee, Lon Mackey. When shall we marry?"

Her frank words shocked a bark of laughter from him.

She turned bright pink. "I shouldn't have said that. *Thee* is supposed to propose to me." She turned even pinker.

He rose and drew her up with him. "Mercy Gabriel, if you recall, I did propose to you, just not for the right reason. I'll marry you as soon as you wish. Today, if you want." He tugged her hand and reveled in folding her into his embrace.

"Not quite today, Lon," she whispered. "But soon. Yes, soon."

For several wonderful moments he held her to him. He loved this woman and she loved him. And he had a future—they had a future together. He kissed her and let the feel of her against him ease the old pain, the old resistance. "Mercy," he murmured.

Someone pounded on the door. "My girl's in labor!" Ma Bailey said from outside the cabin. "You got to come."

Lon couldn't believe it. Did this woman always have to pop up when he least wanted to see her?

Mercy went to the door, brought the older woman inside and helped her sit down. "Thee shouldn't be running like this. When did the labor begin?"

"A few hours ago when you were busy in court."

"Well, first labors usually take longest. I'm sure we'll be in time if we walk." Mercy stopped, frowning, and then said, "Ma, I thought thy son-in-law didn't want a woman doctor attending his wife."

Still panting, Ma grinned. "He's talked to some of the men in town and they all said that you should do it. And today he got a look at that Boise doc, didn't like him and changed his mind. Will you come?"

"I will." Mercy turned to Lon. "I'm afraid, dear one, that I must leave before I have made thee tea."

"That's all right. I'd better get used to this. Marriage to a doctor certainly won't be boring." He grinned the widest and happiest grin he'd ever known.

Ma Bailey whooped with pleasure. "I knew it! I knew you two would make a good match!"

The long hours of labor ended just at dawn. Lon sat at Ma Bailey's kitchen table across from the young father, Aaron Whipple. Lon had kept the gangly young man company through the long hours, making conversation and drinking coffee. At the sound of a baby's cry, Whipple rose from the table, looking stunned and somewhat stupefied. He wobbled a little on his feet.

Lon stood also and gripped the man by his upper arm to steady him.

Then Ma Bailey walked out, beaming. "Come in and meet your son."

Whipple staggered into the room down the hall. Lon held back, but Ma motioned for him to come, too. Lon stayed outside the room but looked in at the new father and mother and the infant in the mother's arms. The sight warmed him to his heart.

His Mercy came to him. He put an arm around her shoulder and pulled her close. His wife-to-be was responsible for this happy outcome—he was certain of that.

"Thanks," the new father said, looking to Mercy. "Thanks, Doc."

"We call her Dr. Mercy around here," Ma Bailey said, looking happier than she ever had before.

Lon knew what the older woman was feeling. He was happier than he could ever remember being. And as long as Mercy was in his life, that happiness would continue. *God, I have been avoiding You for a long time, but no more. Thank You for Your mercy and for my Mercy, too.*

Epilogue

The town east of Idaho Bend was decorated for Christmas. Every store window displayed festive clothing, food or gifts. Lon had driven Mercy, Indigo and Sunny, with her baby girl, Dawn, to meet the train. They stood in the depot, watching for it. The sharp December wind blew against them.

Holding on to his hat, Lon tried to ease the tension that was twisting up his spine. He was about to meet his in-laws for the first time. And since they had left home before he'd married Mercy a few weeks ago, they didn't yet know about Mercy being his wife. They'd had no way to telegraph the news to her parents already in transit.

"My parents will love thee," Mercy said, straightening his collar.

He grinned. He was still a clear pane of glass to his wife. He hoped she was right.

The only touch of sadness was the fact that Pierre

Gauthier had not returned to Idaho Bend. Lon knew that first loves often went astray. For her part, Indigo was still keeping faith that Pierre would return, focusing on waitressing, working on filling her hope chest and helping Mercy.

They heard the train whistle and puffing steam engine. Soon the passengers, mostly people who would be heading farther west, filled the platform and depot.

Mercy shepherded her party toward an older couple dressed in sober black—a tall man with white hair and a petite woman who reminded Lon of Mercy.

"Mother, Father!" Mercy called out. The three took turns embracing and then Mercy turned to Lon and Sunny. "Father and Mother, this is Sunny and her little girl, Dawn."

Adam and Constance Gabriel greeted Sunny warmly, and the young woman curtsied and smiled shyly.

"And this is my husband, Lon Mackey." Mercy blushed at her own words.

There was a moment of wordless surprise. Lon wished he could speak, but his tongue had turned to wood. He wanted to tell them how much he loved their daughter, how her love and God's had healed him. But words failed him.

"Well, welcome to the family, Lon Mackey," Adam said, shaking Lon's hand with a much younger man's vigor. Adam studied Lon, as if delving into him deeply.

"Yes, welcome, Lon Mackey," Constance said, holding up her hands. "Mercy, I don't know what to say. I thought thee had decided never to marry." Mercy's mother smiled at her with a knowing sparkle in her eyes.

"I couldn't marry a man who didn't want me to continue my profession, of course," Mercy said, still rosy pink. "But Lon does and he loves me."

"I am one hundred percent behind Mercy continuing to practice medicine," Lon declared.

"And I am happy to announce that Lon is reading law. I hope he will run for territorial office in the next election." Mercy glowed with joy.

"Excellent!" Adam said, punctuating all the good news. "Mercy, thy mother and I are very tired. Could we go to a hotel?"

The group headed to one of the nearby hotels where Lon and Mercy had already secured rooms for Mercy's parents.

After letting Adam and Constance have a few moments to freshen up, they went to a nearby café. Lon still fought twinges of nerves. So far, Mercy's parents had been welcoming. But an unexpected son-in-law could make a poor impression—he hadn't formally asked Mercy's father for her hand in marriage. Lon didn't know how to rectify this faux pas.

When the waitress delivered their meals, Mercy's father bowed his head and said a brief prayer. The quiet prayer soothed Lon's nerves. He began to sense the natural peace that his in-laws brought with them.

"So thee is the man who has won my eldest daughter's heart," Adam said with a grin.

"Yes, I am the lucky man." Lon suddenly choked up. Truer words had never passed his lips.

"Where is thee from, Lon?" Constance asked.

"Maryland. But I have no family there except for a couple of older aunts and a few cousins. I wrote to them of my marriage, of course."

"I am sorry that thy parents aren't here to share our joy," Constance said, beaming. "We are so happy for thee. I see thy love for our Mercy in thy face."

Creating a small commotion and grabbing everyone's attention, little Dawn cooed and wriggled as if reaching for Constance.

The woman put down her fork and held out her arms for the baby. Sunny hesitated and then complied. Constance talked to the baby with soft, cheery words.

Sunny wiped tears from her eyes. "I'm just so grateful."

Constance laid a comforting hand on Sunny's sleeve. "We are the ones who are grateful. When we offered to come and take thee and thy little one home with us, we didn't know that we would end up meeting our new son-in-law. What a wonderful surprise, such a wonderful blessing. God had it all planned for us."

Lon again felt the deep tug of intense emotion,

of the brilliant truth that radiated from his mother-in-law's simple words. He reached for Mercy and clasped her hand in his. *I couldn't have said it better myself, God. Thank You.*

* * * * *

Dear Readers,

I hope that you have enjoyed reading the stories of these three special sisters, Verity, Felicity and Mercy Gabriel. I've enjoyed doing the historical research for each story and have grown to love these characters.

Very few people have the audacity to go against popular opinion. It takes a special kind of faith and strength. But Mercy needed a support system, too—Indigo, Mercy's new friend, Ellen Dunfield, and, of course, her helpmeet, Lon. As Solomon said in Ecclesiastes 4:11–12a: "…if two lie down together, they will keep warm. But how can one keep warm alone? Though one may be overpowered, two can defend themselves." Two are better than one.

As for Indigo and the other African-American characters in The Gabriel Sisters series, it's hard to believe that it took nearly a hundred years to finally put to rest laws that discriminated against African-Americans in the United States. Though some prejudice lingers in the dark corners of America, our laws no longer uphold it.

Nevertheless, if Verity, Felicity and Mercy walked the streets of the U.S. today, they would still find plenty to keep them busy. I hope that these three sisters will make you sensitive to those who need God's love. I hope they will inspire you to let His light shine in this present darkness.

Please drop by www.strongwomenbravestories.com and www.craftieladiesofromance.blogspot.com for more about stories by me and other Love Inspired authors.

Lyn Cote

QUESTIONS FOR DISCUSSION

1. Have you ever known or talked to a veteran? Have you ever asked him what it was like to come home after a conflict?

2. Do you think that Civil War veterans had struggles similar to those of military personnel today?

3. Do you believe that God has a path or a plan for each life?

4. Why do you think men didn't want women to enter the professions in earlier times?

5. Did you have any women in your family who were ahead of their time? What did they do?

6. Do you know what post-traumatic stress syndrome is? How did this manifest itself in Lon and in Mercy?

7. Why do you think the people of Idaho Bend changed their minds about a woman practicing medicine?

8. Could you travel far from your family to do what God wanted you to?

9. Why do you think the Boise doctor was so angry about Mercy being a doctor?

10. The man who stabbed Lon wanted vengeance. Why is seeking revenge unwise?

11. Why did Lon become a gambler? Do you think he would have continued on this path if he hadn't met Mercy?

12. What was your favorite scene in this book? Why?

13. Have you ever forgiven someone who hurt you or someone you love? How did you feel afterward?

14. Indigo suffered from prejudice. Where do you think prejudice springs from?

15. Do you support any medical missions? If so, which ones? Why?

Love Inspired.
HISTORICAL

TITLES AVAILABLE NEXT MONTH

Available January 11, 2011

REQUEST YOUR FREE BOOKS!

2 FREE INSPIRATIONAL NOVELS
PLUS 2
FREE
MYSTERY GIFTS

Love Inspired
HISTORICAL
INSPIRATIONAL HISTORICAL ROMANCE

YES! Please send me 2 FREE Love Inspired® Historical novels and my 2 FREE mystery gifts (gifts are worth about $10). After receiving them, if I don't wish to receive any more books, I can return the shipping statement marked "cancel". If I don't cancel, I will receive 4 brand-new novels every other month and be billed just $4.24 per book in the U.S. or $4.74 per book in Canada. That's a saving of over 20% off the cover price. It's quite a bargain! Shipping and handling is just 50¢ per book.* I understand that accepting the 2 free books and gifts places me under no obligation to buy anything. I can always return a shipment and cancel at any time. Even if I never buy another book, the two free books and gifts are mine to keep forever.

102/302 IDN E7QD

Name	(PLEASE PRINT)

Address	Apt. #

City	State/Prov.	Zip/Postal Code

Signature (if under 18, a parent or guardian must sign)

Mail to Steeple Hill Reader Service:
IN U.S.A.: P.O. Box 1867, Buffalo, NY 14240-1867
IN CANADA: P.O. Box 609, Fort Erie, Ontario L2A 5X3

Not valid for current subscribers to Love Inspired Historical books.

Want to try two free books from another series?
Call 1-800-873-8635 or visit www.morefreebooks.com.

---

* Terms and prices subject to change without notice. Prices do not include applicable taxes. Sales tax applicable in N.Y. Canadian residents will be charged applicable provincial taxes and GST. Offer not valid in Quebec. This offer is limited to one order per household. All orders subject to approval. Credit or debit balances in a customer's account(s) may be offset by any other outstanding balance owed by or to the customer. Please allow 4 to 6 weeks for delivery. Offer available while quantities last.

Your Privacy: Steeple Hill Books is committed to protecting your privacy. Our Privacy Policy is available online at www.SteepleHill.com or upon request from the Reader Service. From time to time we make our lists of customers available to reputable third parties who may have a product or service of interest to you. If you would prefer we not share your name and address, please check here. ☐

Help us get it right—We strive for accurate, respectful and relevant communications. To clarify or modify your communication preferences, visit us at www.ReaderService.com/consumerschoice.

LIH10R

When Texas Ranger Benjamin Fritz arrives at his captain's house after receiving an urgent message, he finds him murdered and the man's daughter in shock.

Read on for a sneak peek at DAUGHTER OF TEXAS by Terri Reed, the first book in the exciting new TEXAS RANGER JUSTICE series, available January 2011 from Love Inspired Suspense.

Corinna's dark hair had loosened from her normally severe bun. And her dark eyes were glassy as she stared off into space. Taking her shoulders in his hands, Ben pulled her to her feet. She didn't resist. He figured shock was setting in.

When she turned to face him, his heart contracted painfully in his chest. "You're hurt!"

She didn't seem to hear him.

Blood seeped from a scrape on her right upper biceps. He inspected the wound. Looked as if a bullet had grazed her. Whoever had killed her father had tried to kill her. With aching ferocity, rage roared through Ben. The heat of the bullet cauterized the flesh. It would probably heal quickly enough.

But Ben had a feeling that her heart wouldn't heal anytime soon. She'd adored her father. That had been apparent from the moment Ben set foot in the Pike world. She'd barely tolerated Ben from the get-go, with her icy stares and brusque manner, making it clear she thought him not good enough to be in her world. But when it came to her father...

Greg had known that if anything happened to him, she'd need help coping with the loss.

Ben, I need you to promise me if anything ever happens to me, you'll watch out for Corinna. She'll need an anchor.

I fear she's too fragile to suffer another death.

Of course Ben had promised. Though he'd refused to even allow the thought to form that any harm would befall his mentor and friend. He'd wanted to believe Greg was indestructible. But he wasn't. None of them were.

The Rangers were human and very mortal, performing a risky job that put their lives on the line every day.

Never before had Ben been so acutely aware of that fact.

Now his captain was gone. It was up to him not only to bring Greg's murderer to justice, but to protect and help Corinna Pike.

*For more of this story, look for DAUGHTER OF TEXAS
by Terri Reed, available in January 2011
from Love Inspired Suspense.*

Love Inspired

Bestselling author

JILLIAN HART

brings readers another heartwarming story
from

the

GRANGER
FAMILY
RANCH

To fulfill a sick boy's wish, rodeo star Tucker Granger surprises
little Owen in the hospital. And no one is more surprised than
single mother Sierra Baker. But somehow Tucker ropes her heart
and fills it with hope. Hope that this country girl and her son
can lasso the roaming bronc rider into their family forever.

Look for

His Country Girl

*Available January
wherever books are sold.*

www.SteepleHill.com

Steeple
Hill®

LI87643

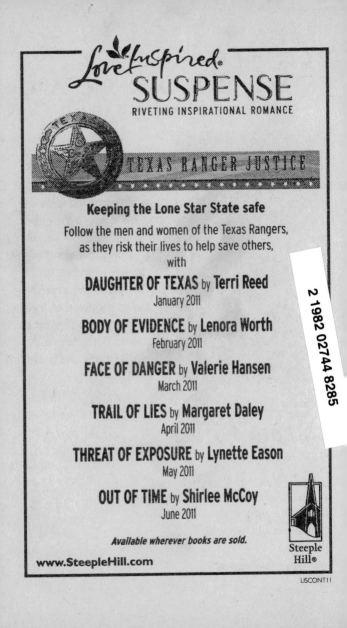